JAMES PATTERSON is one of the best-known and biggest-selling writers of all time. His books have sold in excess of 325 million copies worldwide. He is the author of some of the most popular series of the past two decades – the Alex Cross, Women's Murder Club, Detective Michael Bennett and Private novels – and he has written many other number one bestsellers including romance novels and stand-alone thrillers.

James is passionate about encouraging children to read. Inspired by his own son who was a reluctant reader, he also writes a range of books for young readers including the Middle School, I Funny, Treasure Hunters, House of Robots, Confessions and Maximum Ride series. James has donated millions in grants to independent bookshops and he has been the most borrowed author in UK libraries for the past ten years in a row. He lives in Florida with his wife and son.

BOOK**SHOTS**

STORIES AT THE SPEED OF LIFE

What you are holding in your hands right now is no ordinary book, it's a BookShot.

BookShots are page-turning stories by James Patterson and other writers that can be read in one sitting.

Each and every one is fast-paced, 100% story-driven; a shot of pure entertainment guaranteed to satisfy.

Available as new, compact paperbacks, ebooks and audio, everywhere books are sold.

BookShots – the ultimate form of storytelling. From the ultimate storyteller.

DEADLY CARGO

JAMES PATTERSON

WITH WILL JORDAN

BOOKSHOTS

3 5 7 9 10 8 6 4 2

BookShots
20 Vauxhall Bridge Road
London SW1V 2SA

BookShots is part of the Penguin Random House group of companies
whose addresses can be found at global.penguinrandomhouse.com.

First published by BookShots in 2017

www.penguin.co.uk

A CIP catalogue record for this book is available
from the British Library.

ISBN 9781786531766

Typeset in Garamond Premier Pro font 11/15.5 pt by Jouve (UK), Milton Keynes
Printed and bound in Great Britain by Clays Ltd, St Ives Plc

DEADLY CARGO

CHAPTER 1

Freighter M.V. Ossora, *Bering Sea – 1240 nautical miles west of Anchorage, Alaska*

NIGHT HAD FALLEN ON the frigid stretch of water that lay between Alaska and the eastern tip of Russia, the weak disc of the sun disappearing behind dark ominous clouds that seemed to stretch across the whole western horizon. The sea beneath this overcast sky was a roiling mass of dark waves and churning foam, whipped up by strong winds howling in from the north.

And it was through this stormy weather that the massive bulk of the M.V. *Ossora* floundered slowly southward, rolling and pitching in the heavy seas as powerful waves crashed against her rusted bow. Every once in a while her single propeller would roar as the ship's roll lifted it right out of the water, only to crash back down amidst a torrent of churning foam.

A relic of the days when the hammer and sickle still flew over the Kremlin, she had been designed without the slightest consideration for aesthetics or comfort – her hull was wide and squat, her bow blunt and uncompromising, her superstructure little more than a gigantic white box streaked with corrosion. Now almost forty years old and suffering from neglect by a company unwilling to scrap her but unable to overhaul her, she required the combined efforts of her entire engineering staff just to stay running.

These matters were of little to concern to Leonid Ivanov however as he hurried down a narrow corridor lit by flickering electric lights, its yellowed walls and ceiling testimony to the countless sailors who had passed this way with cigarettes in hand. Turning right, he ascended a steep flight of steps to the next deck, silently cursing as the ship's roll threatened to pitch him backward.

Clutching at a handrail, Ivanov waited a few moments while the vessel temporarily stabilized before resuming his climb, intent on reaching his destination.

The ship's bridge was, in contrast to the rest of the dilapidated vessel, a haven of order and cleanliness, its navigation and communications equipment carefully maintained. He might have been in charge of a run-down cargo tub destined for the breaker's yard, but Captain Nikolaev took his responsibility as ship's master seriously.

The atmosphere in the control room was tense and silent as Ivanov entered. Men were hunched over navigation consoles and chart tables, or peering out into the freezing darkness as if they could pierce the gloom beyond their vessel through willpower alone. The air was heavy with cigarette smoke and fraught nerves.

Nikolaev himself was standing near the ship's wheel, surveying the radar plot with a grim, unhappy expression. A bear of a man who must have been seventy if he was a day, Nikolaev was an old navy veteran who had long since moved into commercial shipping. He was soft spoken and reserved for the most part, radiating a silent calm and rarely raising his voice in anger. When he did, however, he was a force to behold. Ivanov had seen more than one outspoken sailor cower before his wrath.

"Captain," Ivanov began.

Several pairs of eyes turned to him, then quickly glanced away again as the bridge crew resumed their difficult task of navigating the *Ossora* through rough seas. A lowly cargo handler, Ivanov wasn't important enough to warrant their attention.

"What is it, Leonid?" Nikolaev asked, stirring from his ruminations.

Ivanov moved closer and lowered his voice. "Sorry to disturb you, sir, but I need to show you something. In the cargo bay."

The captain's thick graying brows drew together in a frown. "We have a storm bearing down on us, son. Unless the ship's in danger, I'm needed here."

Reaching out, Ivanov grabbed the older man's arm. "Sir, it's about the cargo containers. I think . . . I think there's something in them that shouldn't be. I don't trust anyone else but you."

Nikolaev stared back at the young sailor, comprehension dawning on him. Seconds passed, broken by the patter of rain and sea spray lashing against the bridge windows.

"Chief, take over here," Nikolaev said abruptly, addressing the ship's first officer, before turning back to Ivanov. "All right, son. Show me."

It took about five minutes for Ivanov and the elderly captain to make their way down from the bridge to one of the *Ossora*'s two cavernous cargo holds. Nikolaev was as sure footed as a mountain goat and knew the ship from bow to stern, but he was also a big man who wisely moved with caution. He'd lost more than one crewman in his time to a careless slip down a stairwell in high seas.

Much of Number One Hold's internal space was given over to big steel shipping containers, holding everything from engine parts to computer components and mass-produced clothing, their careful arrangement to balance the ship's load resembling a stack of giant Lego bricks. Illumination was provided by a few weak overhead floodlights, a couple of which were out of action, leaving the hold bathed in gloom.

"You're sure of what you heard?" Nikolaev asked as the two men halted before one container in particular. Checking the container number, the captain held up a flashlight and surveyed the cargo manifest he'd brought with him. "According to this, it holds water pumping equipment."

This was his last chance to back out, Ivanov knew. To force open a container without the owner's permission would involve a breach of their shipping contract, and likely result in severe financial penalties for them all.

"I'm sure, sir," he said after a moment.

The captain chewed on it for a few seconds, before finally nodding his assent. "Very well. Open it up."

Like most the other containers, Number 29 was secured with a steel padlock to prevent tampering or theft of its contents. However, the pair of heavy bolt cutters Ivanov brought with him made easy work of the hardened steel shackle. Removing the defeated lock, Ivanov yanked upward on the container's securing bolt, held his breath and swung the thick metal door open.

The moment Nikolaev's flashlight beam played across the interior of the container, illuminating its contents, the old man's mouth dropped open in shock.

"Oh my God," Ivanov gasped.

CHAPTER 2

Casco Cove Coast Guard Station, Attu Island

"SHIT," LIEUTENANT RICK O'NEILL growled, watching the slowly expanding patch of red on his chin as it blended with the white of shaving foam.

The light above the mirror in his washroom was defective, flickering on and off seemingly at random. As a result, his daily shave had become a clandestine affair: using the brief moments of visibility he ran the razor over as much skin as possible before the bulb gave out again. But with haste came mistakes, as his father had once said.

One of the few bits of useful advice the man ever gave him.

Sighing, he dabbed at the bleeding cut. He leaned forward, looking at his reflection in the steamed mirror. Even features, a clean jawline, a straight nose, eyes that were the same gray-blue as a stormy sea, dark hair still shiny and wet from the shower. Thirty-eight years old, and going nowhere fast.

The light flickered, struggled vainly to stay lit, then went out again.

Satisfied that he'd done what he could, he walked through to his living quarters, wiping off the last of the soap from his face and pressing the wash towel against his chin to help stop the bleeding. The place smelled of dust and old leather and age. Like his washroom light and everything else on this lonely U.S. Coast Guard station at the end of the world, it was faded and worn out and overdue for retirement.

Casco Cove was scheduled to be decommissioned in six months or so, but for the time being the Coast Guard maintained a tenuous presence here. A skeleton staff kept the island's only runway up and running, allowing supplies and equipment to be flown in, while a single 47-foot MLB (Motor Life Boat) sat in a covered maintenance shed ready to be launched in the event of an emergency.

And in charge of this graveyard operation was O'Neill himself. Well, for now at least.

Slipping on the dark blue shirt of his operational dress uniform, the standard Coast Guard uniform used for day to day work, O'Neill straightened up, took a deep breath and opened his door.

A short walk brought him to the station's ops room, nominally the hub of all activity on the base, but today resembling a deserted office. Only two personnel were on duty at such a late hour, neither of whom looked particularly engaged in their work.

O'Neill couldn't blame them. This far from the major shipping lanes, the most excitement they had around these parts was the monthly supply flight from Anchorage.

"You've been in the wars," Ensign Wyatt Richards remarked from behind his satellite communications terminal.

Short, stocky, and with his receding hairline shaved almost to the scalp, he was a couple of months away from leaving the Coast Guard. He was intelligent and competent enough, but had no real ambition to get anywhere in the service, which was probably why he'd ended up here. He'd joined because the Coast Guard offered an easy way to get his ship pilot qualifications.

"Cut myself shaving," O'Neill said.

"What do you shave with? A bread knife?" O'Neill flashed him a warning look, which prompted a blush to rise to his otherwise pale face. "Sorry, forget I said anything."

"Already done," O'Neill assured him. "Now, what's our status?"

Richards shrugged. "All clear across the board. No contacts, no active incidents to report."

O'Neill sighed and looked around, taking in the largely inactive ops room. This was as good a place as any to make the announcement. "Where are Watkins and Rodriguez?"

The other two members of his station detail, Bryce Watkins and Sebastian "Seb" Rodriguez were as thick as thieves and rarely to be found apart. Not that there were many places to go in such an isolated posting.

At this, the second officer on duty piped up from the other side of the ops room. "Saw them in the rec room about half an hour ago, sir."

Kate Starke was, in contrast to Richards, a bright and promising young Petty Officer who just happened to have drawn a bad hand with her posting here. Still, she appeared to have accepted the unenviable assignment without complaint, which put her well up in O'Neill's estimation. Successfully completing a tour in a place like Attu Island without going mad would bode well for her chances of promotion later.

O'Neill nodded, his mind now made up. "Would you have them come to the ops room in fifteen minutes?"

"Of course."

Richards frowned, sensing something out of sorts in O'Neill's demeanor. "Everything okay, sir?"

"Just make sure they're here. I'll be in my office until then," he said, turning away and striding from the room.

CHAPTER 3

Therefore, I hereby resign my commission as an officer in the United States Coast Guard, effective immediately. Please make arrangements for my transportation back to Anchorage, and for a replacement CO to take over this station as soon as convenient.

Yours sincerely,

Lieutenant Richard O'Neill, U.S.C.G.

O'NEILL STARED AT THE words on the computer screen—not much to say for a ten-year career in the service, but there it was. The message was written, and a single mouse click would send it off to Coast Guard Headquarters in Washington, D.C.

He was done with the job. Even after this station was decommissioned, he knew the rest of his career would be assignments just like this one. He'd never again serve where it mattered, and would certainly never get to command his own ship. He'd rather have nothing, make a clean break and start a new life. Maybe he'd follow Richards' example and get into commercial shipping.

As soon as the message was sent off, he'd make the announcement to the small team under his command. He doubted any of them would shed tears over his departure. He'd hardly been a barrel of fun since his move here three months ago, and had done little to endear himself to the personnel on base. At best they dutifully obeyed his commands without enthusiasm, and at worst they were openly defiant.

He took another drink of whiskey, grimacing as it lit a fire inside him. It was good stuff – strong, rich, and fairly expensive. But it brought him no comfort tonight.

He was about to send the message when there came a knock at his door. Frowning, he quickly minimized the email window.

"Come!" he called, not bothering to put his jacket back on.

The door opened, and to his surprise, Starke was standing there.

O'Neill rose from his chair. "What can I do for you, Starke?"

"I was wondering if I could . . . have a word, sir. In private."

O'Neill frowned, but beckoned for her to come forward. "All right. Come in."

She stepped over the threshold and closed the door behind her, then just stood there, looking around with a mixture of curiosity and a hint of sadness, as if she could see O'Neill's predecessors mourning what had become of their quarters.

"You said you wanted to talk," he prompted.

"Permission to speak freely."

He almost wanted to laugh. "We're not in the Navy. Say what's on your mind."

The young woman took a deep breath and raised her chin a little. "What's going on, sir? If we've done something . . ."

"You haven't."

"Then what's wrong?"

O'Neill sighed. Unlike most of the others, she actually seemed to give a shit about his mental state. "Take a seat."

The young woman walked over to the worn leather seating area and lowered herself down, as if testing whether it would hold her weight. O'Neill refilled his glass and held the bottle up. "Drink?"

"Aren't you still on duty?"

He shrugged and took a sip. "Won't matter soon." He sat on the edge of his desk and looked at her for a moment. "Let me ask you something. You always want to be in the service?"

She thought about it for a moment, then nodded. "I guess so."

"Why?"

The young woman was quiet, as if deciding how much to tell him. "My dad was a fisherman, worked as a pilot on a trawler off the Grand Banks," she said, apparently deciding to open up a little. "One night they got caught up in a squall and their generator quit on them, pretty much killed the whole boat dead as a rock. They were getting hit with forty-foot waves and taking on water when the Coast Guard managed to get a boat out and towed them back to port. When my dad told them they could have been pulled under too if the trawler sank, the boat commander said, 'That's our job, sir. We have to go out' . . ."

"But we don't have to come back," O'Neill finished for her, quoting the Coast Guard's informal motto.

She grinned and nodded. "Right then I was hooked. I thought anyone with that kind of attitude was badass, and I wanted to be like that. And . . . well, it seemed more fun than working in some office building somewhere."

O'Neill smiled at the irony of that one, glancing at the rain lashing against his window. A storm was brewing outside; a common occurrence at this time of year. "Well, you got your wish, I guess."

"Not everyone in the Air Force gets to fly fighter jets," she said, sensing his unspoken thoughts. "Doesn't mean they're not useful."

He said nothing to that.

"Now you know about me," she reminded him. "You still haven't answered my question. What's going on?"

O'Neill looked at the drink in his hand. But before he could say anything further, the intercom on his desk buzzed, its tone harsh and demanding. Setting down his drink, O'Neill yanked the chunky receiver out of its cradle. "Yeah?"

"Sir, it's Richards. I think you'd better get to the ops room right now." There was an excited, almost panicked edge to the man's voice that O'Neill had never heard before. "We've got a distress call."

"On my way."

O'Neill swore under his breath as he replaced the phone and rose from his desk, gulping down the remainder of his glass. Richards' timing couldn't have been worse.

CHAPTER 4

THE OPS ROOM WAS a hive of excited chatter as O'Neill strode into the room, closely followed by Starke. The other two members of his team had apparently answered their summons to report for duty, though it was clear from their uncharacteristic looks of interest that there was something else at play now.

Rodriguez was the first to catch his eye. Tall and heavily muscled, he had the V-shaped physique of a bodybuilder and the attitude to match. He was a rescue diver by profession, trained to drop via chopper and pull survivors from the water before they froze to death. O'Neill hadn't yet seen him in action, but if his bragging was anything to go by, he was truly a force to be reckoned with.

His colleague Bryce Watkins on the other hand was a slope-shouldered, spare-looking man in his forties, who constantly projected an air of being put-upon. His thinning hair was slicked back to hide a growing bald spot, his narrow face pockmarked by teenage acne, his expression usually alternating between surly disrespect and thinly veiled mockery.

"Talk to me, Wyatt," O'Neill commanded. "What's going on?"

Richards, manning the comms station, pulled away his headset long enough to speak. "Got a Russian freighter in trouble, sir," he explained hurriedly. "The M.V. *Ossora*, two days out of Magadan. They've lost main engine power, and backup generators are failing. According to their last transmission, they're taking on water and might not have the power to keep broadcasting much longer. They've requested assistance to repair their engines."

"Maybe if they kept a decent mechanic onboard we wouldn't have to come save their useless asses," Watkins snorted.

"Keep your opinions to yourself, Mr Watkins," O'Neill warned with a sharp look. "How long ago did they put out a distress call?"

"About thirty minutes. Took a while for HQ to filter it through to us. They're trying to raise them again, but there's been no further contact."

"And what do we know about the *Ossora*?"

Richards had at least been switched-on enough to pull up the ship's registry data. "Russian multipurpose cargo carrier, first registered in nineteen seventy-two. Displacement is about seven thousand five hundred tonnes fully loaded. Standard crew complement is fourteen."

"Be surprised if they have half that number," Rodriguez remarked cynically. Captains of small commercial freighters were known to run with skeleton crews to save money.

O'Neill hurried over to the nearby chart table. "What's her position and heading?"

"Erm . . ." Richards began shuffling through the printed report he'd received from Coast Guard regional HQ in Anchorage.

"Take your time, Wyatt," Watkins said mockingly as the young ensign fumbled for the information.

"Bite my ass, Watkins." At last finding what he was looking for, Richards snatched up the emergency dispatch. "Last reported position was . . . fifty-five degrees, forty minutes north. One hundred and seventy-five degrees, fifty-six minutes east. Heading is unknown; she's just drifting."

O'Neill studied the charts for several seconds, plotting out the latitude and longitude. "That's about sixty miles north of here. She'll be drifting south-east with the current." Another blast of wind hit the window so hard that it rattled in its frame. "That's at the edge of our effective range. Signal the *Munro* and advise her of their situation. We're in no shape to go out in this weather."

U.S.C.G.C. *Munro* was a Hamilton-class high-endurance Coast Guard cutter, charged with patrolling the icy waters of the Bering Sea and the Gulf of Alaska. Nearly four hundred feet long and with a crew of over a hundred and fifty, she was far better placed to conduct a rescue operation than a five-man motor patrol craft.

Richards' expression told him the news wasn't good. "Already tried her, sir. She was diverted north to help a factory ship in trouble off the coast. It'll be dawn before she gets here." He made an almost apologetic gesture. "We're the only station in range."

Silence descended on the room then, broken only by the faint pop and crackle of Richards' headset, and the lashing rain and sleet against the window. O'Neill could feel all eyes on him, particularly Starke's. Glancing up from the chart table at the young woman, he saw her look of confusion and dismay. She couldn't understand why he was so reluctant to act.

God damn it, he thought, silently cursing the timing of such an emergency.

"Well, then it's up to us," he conceded at last. "Mr Rodriguez, prep the MLB for launch. Mr Richards, advise regional command we're en route now. And keep trying to raise the *Ossora* on the emergency band. Everyone else, prep your gear. We leave in five minutes."

"Are you kidding me, sir?" Watkins asked. "Look outside your window. We've got a Force nine storm coming our way. We're not set up for this kind of—"

"You have your orders, Mr Watkins," O'Neill interrupted, rounding on the reluctant engineer. "Are you going to obey them or not?"

Watkins eyed him darkly for a long moment. "Aye, aye. Sir," he said with barely concealed sarcasm.

Holding his gaze a second longer, O'Neill finally turned away, directing his attention to the chart table so he could plot a search area for the *Ossora*.

"Lighten up, Watkins," Rodriguez advised his companion. "We have to go out. We don't have to—"

"Don't fucking say it," Watkins called over his shoulder as he strode off to retrieve his wet-weather gear.

CHAPTER 5

"JESUS," STARKE MUMBLED, BRACING herself against the console as their fifty-foot-long motor lifeboat crested another big wave, the bow tilting dangerously downward before righting itself in a cloud of spray and foam. Rain continued to lash the windshield as the boat powered onward at twenty-five knots, reducing visibility despite the wipers working overtime.

"This is some shitty weather we've got, skipper," Richards remarked with a worried frown, visibly pale now as the deck rocked and pitched beneath him.

O'Neill, manning the ship's wheel, shrugged as he stared out across the darkened, storm-tossed sea illuminated by the craft's powerful search-lights. "It's going to get worse before it gets better. Satellite tracking says we've got a storm coming from the north. This is the leading edge of it."

"You sure we can even make it in this thing?" Richards asked.

"She's designed to survive sixty-knot winds and twenty-foot waves," O'Neill said, increasing power as the bow rose skyward and the boat tackled another towering wave. "Beyond that . . . your guess is as good as mine."

Richards swallowed hard, looking like he was about to throw up.

"You got anything on radar?" O'Neill asked.

Starke scanned her scope. "Nothing yet. There's too much surface clutter with all these waves. You sure this is the right area?"

The commander glanced at her. "Assuming the position they gave was accurate, they should have drifted with the current and ended up somewhere around here."

Richards glanced at the fuel readouts. A third of their reserve had been used up just getting out to the search area. "We can't stay here more than an hour or we'll be swimming home, sir."

"Then we'd better hope we find them, hadn't we, Richards?"

"I'm telling you, man. The guy's bad fucking news," Watkins said as he leaned over to check the oil pressure on the starboard diesel engine, having to shout to be heard above the din. "Why the hell do you think someone like him got posted out here in the first place?"

"How the hell should I know?" Rodriguez fired back. "Maybe he likes peace and quiet."

"Nah, there's more to it than that—you mark my words, boy." Glancing towards the hatch leading forward to make sure it was still secured, he added, "I've got a buddy in Anchorage. He says the word is that O'Neill got one of his crew killed, but he was too well connected to be discharged so they sent him out here until it all died down."

"I'm calling bullshit on that, dude," Rodriguez scoffed.

"Call it what you want, but I sure as hell ain't turning my back on that guy."

Occupied in conversation, they failed to hear the click as the hatch was opened behind them, and whirled around in surprise to see Starke standing there braced against the bulkhead. She was watching them with the kind of wary distrust that suggested she'd heard more than they'd intended.

"Hey, Kate," Rodriguez said innocently. "You need something?"

She eyed the two men a moment longer before speaking. "Skipper wants a fuel status update, and you're not answering your comms."

"Would you look at that?" Watkins said, checking the intercom unit mounted on the wall and turning the volume dial back up. "Must have switched it off without realizing."

"Might want to keep an eye on that in future," the young woman advised.

"Will do," Watkins agreed, smiling at her without warmth. "Anything else?"

No doubt she was aware of the hostility radiating from him, but to her credit she appeared unshaken by it.

The uneasy standoff was broken only when the intercom crackled into life with O'Neill's voice. "Starke, get up to the bridge now. Acknowledge."

Keeping her eyes on Watkins, Starke reached out and hit the bridge transmit button on the unit. "On my way."

"Better run. Captain's calling," Watkins said, his tone faintly mocking as she unlatched the hatch and stepped out of the engine room.

"Watch yourself, Watkins. No telling who might overhear you," Starke advised, before swinging the hatch closed behind her.

"Bitch," Watkins mumbled, resuming his work.

CHAPTER 6

BY THE TIME STARKE had clambered up the gangway to the boat's enclosed bridge and glanced out the window, it was obvious enough why O'Neill had summoned her here.

About a mile directly ahead, partially lit by the dim orange glow of her recognition lights, lay the massive bulk of the M.V. *Ossora.* The big freighter was still too distant for her to make out details, but judging by the movement of her lights, she was stationary and swaying slowly in the rough seas.

"M.V. *Ossora*, M.V. *Ossora*. This is U.S. Coast Guard vessel off your port beam, hailing you on emergency channel," O'Neill spoke into the radio. "Acknowledge this transmission."

His hail was met by the pop and crackle of static.

"Repeat, this is U.S. Coast Guard vessel responding to your distress call. If you cannot respond verbally, acknowledge with Morse lamp or a horn blast."

Nothing. O'Neill's face was etched with concern now.

"Maybe their radio's down," Richards suggested.

"They still have power," Starke pointed out. "If they can see us, they should be able to signal somehow."

Richards checked his radar, where the hull of the big ship showed as a bright splash across the screen. "Range down to eight hundred yards and closing, sir."

O'Neill chewed on it for a moment or two before replacing the radiophone in its cradle. "Reduce speed to ten knots. We're going in for a closer look," he decided. "Starke, light her up."

Flicking on the powerful searchlights mounted topside, Starke watched as the twin beams illuminated the big vessel directly ahead. Towering black walls of steel streaked with rust rose up from the rough sea, giving way to a blunt, crude-looking bow that seemed designed to force its way through the water by sheer brute strength. On deck, the great booms of cranes mounted forward and aft hovered unmoving above the cargo holds, while behind them sat the discolored white box-like superstructure that housed the bridge and crew accommodation.

Aside from a few running lights along the deck and mastheads, there was no sign of life aboard the vessel.

"Range down to two hundred," Richards said as they closed in.

O'Neill's gaze was fixed straight ahead. "Steady as she goes."

"Big ship," Starke remarked, amazed that a vessel of this size could be operated by such a small crew. No wonder they'd run into trouble.

Resuming his position at the radio, O'Neill switched it over to external loudspeaker and tried his hail again. "M.V. *Ossora*, this is U.S. Coast Guard vessel approaching on your port beam, responding to distress call. Stand by to receive boarding party. Acknowledge by radio or visual signal now."

To no one's surprise, there was no response from the vessel.

"Where the hell is everyone?" Richards asked, clearly unnerved by the lack of communication. "Those floodlights must be visible from ten miles away."

"Maybe the crew abandoned ship," Starke suggested, though such an action would make little sense. The *Ossora* might have been robbed of engine power, but there was no obvious sign that she was listing or taking on water.

O'Neill shook his head. "They'd have to be desperate to bail out in this sea." He pointed up to the superstructure, where the portside lifeboat was still securely attached to its launching rail. "Anyway, at least one of the lifeboats is still aboard."

"One hundred yards," Richards reported.

"Bring us up alongside. Looks like there's an access ladder amidships," O'Neill said, indicating a set of steel rungs protruding from the hull. Ascending to the deck in weather like this wasn't going to be much fun, but with no crew answering their hails it seemed there was little choice.

As Richards altered course to port, O'Neill hit his intercom. "Crew, stand by for boarding duty. Gear up.

"Starke, with me," O'Neill said, opening the hatch to venture outside. Straight away a chill gust of wind whipped through the bridge, accompanied by a spray of rain and seawater. "Might want to button up."

Zipping up her waterproof jacket and pulling the hood close, Starke followed the skipper out onto the exposed bridge positioned slightly above and behind them.

The cold hit her straight away, icy blasts of wind howling in from the north and carrying with them a mixture of sleet and rain that chilled any exposed skin within seconds. The towering bulk of the *Ossora* was now perilously close, looming over them like some ancient behemoth poised to crush them beneath its weight.

"Let's go!" O'Neill said, moving down to the starboard deck and lowering a couple of fenders over the side to absorb the impact when they made contact.

Starke followed him, clutching the guard rail tight. The MLB was pitching and rolling hard in the rough seas, though fortunately the bulk of the Russian freighter was helping to shield them from the worst of the weather.

Like O'Neill, Starke was wearing a life jacket and thermally insulated wet-weather gear that would provide a degree of warmth even when submerged, but she was under no illusions about their chances if they went overboard. Life expectancy in this frigid water was down to mere minutes.

They were moving roughly parallel to the ship's hull as Richards inched them cautiously closer. She could see his anxious expression through the bridge windows as he fought with the wheel and throttle controls. Even a collision at low speed could severely damage their boat in such rough conditions.

O'Neill meanwhile was standing by with a grapple hook and line attached to a deck-mounted winch, ready to throw it as the ladder came into range. Starke tensed up as their target edged closer, silently praying he didn't miss. Such a failure would mean circling around to take another run at it.

With a single deft movement, O'Neill hurled the grappling hook, which bounced off the hull between two rungs and lodged firmly around the lower one. Straight away Starke turned to Richards in the enclosed bridge and drew her fingers across her throat, signaling him to cut engine power.

As the MLB throttled down, O'Neill hit the winch. The line to the grapple hook rose up out of the water, then grew taut as it pulled the Coast Guard boat in towards the *Ossora*'s hull. A sudden bump told Starke they had made contact and were now firmly anchored against the target vessel.

Turning towards her, O'Neill gave her a nod, then reached for the radio unit fixed to his shoulder. "Rodriguez, Watkins, on deck."

"Copy that. Should we open up the small arms locker?" Rodriguez asked.

O'Neill hesitated, saying nothing. Starke frowned in surprise, wondering what was troubling him.

"Skipper?" Rodriguez repeated. "Weapons?"

"Very well," O'Neill said at last. "Bring them up."

CHAPTER 7

"UGLY OLD BITCH, AIN'T she?" Watkins remarked, staring at the rust-streaked hull rising up into the darkness above them. His thinning hair was plastered to his head by the rain and wind, but oddly the cold seemed not to trouble him.

"Let's just get this done," O'Neill said, inserting a magazine into the SIG P229 automatic pistol and allowing the slide to move forward, drawing the first round into the breech. The familiar click of the feed mechanism at work sent a chill of foreboding through him that he did his best to ignore.

After checking the safety was engaged, O'Neill slipped the weapon into his hip-mounted holster and made sure the guard flap was locked down. The last thing he wanted was for the weapon to come loose and tumble into the sea during his ascent.

Starke and Watkins were similarly armed with SIG automatics, while Rodriguez was busy loading shells into a Remington pump-action shotgun. Between them, the four-man boarding party had enough firepower to handle just about anything that was likely to be thrown at them. Hopefully it wouldn't come to that.

Firing up his radio once more, O'Neill spoke into it. "Radio check.

Richards, stand by on the MLB and be ready to send out a distress call if we raise the alarm."

"Copy that, skipper," came the crackly reply.

"Lucky bastard," Rodriguez said with a wry grin. "Keep the coffee warm for us, asshole."

"Remember, weapons are for *defense* only," O'Neill added, giving Watkins a warning look. "Do not fire unless fired upon. And watch yourselves during the ascent—move slow and careful. I don't want anyone falling overboard. Everyone clear?"

He was met with a round of affirmatives.

Venturing across the deck, O'Neill gripped the first rung of the ladder and tested his weight on it. Like the rest of the ship, the ladder was marked by corrosion, especially around the welding points, but seemed solid.

With this thought weighing on his mind, O'Neill began his ascent, moving slowly and deliberately, testing each rung before trusting his weight to it. The rocking movement of the ship constantly changed his angle of ascent, occasionally taking it beyond vertical so that he was left with little choice but to hook his feet in and wait for the vessel to stabilize.

Nonetheless, the ladder remained sound, and he was able to make his ascent without incident. Scrambling up onto the midships deck about thirty seconds later, he drew the SIG automatic and swept the area.

As he'd expected, the place was deserted. Both big cargo doors were closed and locked; apart from a few running lights, the place was in darkness. The only noise coming from the vessel was the clank and rattle of chains high up in the crane winch machinery overhead as they swayed with the motion of the waves.

"US Coast Guard!" he shouted, not expecting a reply. "Anyone on board?"

Rodriguez was up next, quickly followed by Starke and Watkins. Unhooking their flashlights, they scanned the immediate vicinity, their beams illuminating neglected deck fixtures and spots of rain and sleet whipping across the ship.

"Real garden spot," Rodriguez remarked.

"Fucking ghost ship, man," Watkins added. "Place is like a tomb."

Ignoring his grim assessment, O'Neill nodded towards the superstructure. "The bridge is this way. Let's go."

Ascending a flight of stairs leading to the portside hatch, the boarding party paused for a moment with weapons ready as Rodriguez gripped the locking mechanism, rain dripping from his wet-weather gear. At a nod from O'Neill, he spun the wheel over and swung the hatch outward, allowing the team to make entry.

The companionway beyond was barely any better maintained than the ship's exterior. Cigarette butts and other minor debris littered the floor, and the place was illuminated only by the dim red glow of emergency lights. Clearly the ship's generators were no longer functioning. Still, at least it was dry and, compared to the freezing winds outside, relatively warm.

"Anybody home?" Watkins called out, his voice echoing eerily down the empty corridor before returning to them a moment later.

O'Neill exchanged a look with Starke but said nothing. Picking his way down the corridor with the rest of the party in tow, he reached an open hatch on his right. Beyond it lay the ship's mess hall: a narrow compartment with a pair of long tables taking up most of the internal space, and a small kitchen area at the far end. He could still smell the lingering odor of tobacco and greasy food in the air.

The team's flashlight beams illuminated a couple of coffee cups sitting on the nearest table, as if their owners had stood up and departed mere moments before the team arrived. Removing his glove, O'Neill dipped his finger in one. It was stone cold.

"Nobody's been here for a while," he decided.

Starke looked around the abandoned room, frowning. "I don't get it. If the crew didn't bail out in a lifeboat, where the hell did they go?"

"Place is a goddamn *Mary Celeste*. Never seen anything like it," Rodriguez said, his voice uncharacteristically hushed. "This is some *X-Files* bullshit here."

"Pussy," Watkins taunted him.

"Who are you calling a pussy?"

"Knock it off, both of you," O'Neill interrupted before their exchange turned into a full-scale argument. "We're here and we've got a job to do. Move on."

Retreating from the mess hall, they continued down the corridor until they reached what looked like a central stairwell that cut through the core of the ship. Below lay the engine rooms and machine spaces, while up above at the top of the superstructure was the ship's bridge.

Leaning over the guard rail, O'Neill peered down the poorly lit stairwell to the bottom of the shaft, several decks below. Like everything else they'd seen so far, there was no sign of life down there.

Searching the entire vessel from bow to stern with a four-man boarding party would take hours. Anyway, that wasn't their only concern. Even if there was currently no explanation for the missing crew, they still had to deal with a ship that was drifting without power or navigation. Something had to be done to bring it under control.

"Okay, we split up," he decided. "Starke and I will work our way up to the bridge, see if there's any clues there. Watkins, you and Rodriguez get down below, assess the status of the engines and report back to me. We need those generators back up."

Without waiting for a response, he clicked the transmit button on his radio. "Richards, what's your status?"

"Taking a pounding out here," Richards replied. "This weather's getting worse. I'm worried we're going to part our mooring line."

"Copy that. Hang tight, we're going to try to get the power back up."

"Any sign of the crew?"

"Nothing yet," O'Neill confirmed. "Looks like she's been abandoned."

"Roger. Standing by."

Clicking the radio off, O'Neill turned to the others. "Okay, let's get this done. Move slow, keep your eyes open and call out anything if you see it. Questions?"

"When can we get off this old tub?" Watkins asked cynically.

"When our job's done," O'Neill replied. "Now get going."

CHAPTER 8

GRIPPING THE SIG AUTOMATIC tight, O'Neill advanced out of the stairwell and onto the *Ossora*'s bridge. Like the rest of the ship's internal spaces, the room was bathed only in the dull red glow of emergency lighting, its navigation consoles blank and its instrument panels powered down. Without mains power, the equipment in this room offered no control over the vessel, and few clues as to its current status. Outside in the darkness, rain continued to lash against the windows.

"Weird seeing a ship's bridge like this," Starke said, surveying the deserted room.

O'Neill was about to move deeper into the room, but stopped, alerted by a familiar smell lingering in the air. Not the scent of tobacco or coffee, but something stronger and acrid. He was willing to bet it was the smell of burned cordite.

"Watch yourself, Starke," he advised, treading carefully as he moved over to the chart table, searching amongst the various maps and navigation documents until he found what he was looking for.

By law, a ship's logbook had to be carried and maintained by the crew of any large vessel, but there were actually two versions kept aboard for the sake of convenience. The "rough log" was filled out every few hours by the chief officer of the watch, recording the ship's speed, position, and heading, as well as any notable events. Given that such entries depended on the diligence of the officer on duty, rough logs could vary considerably in detail and quality. Only later was this hastily written information transcribed by the captain into the official logbook, known as the "smooth log."

In this case, however, the rough log was preferable as it was generally the most up to date. Laying the large notebook down on the chart table, O'Neill flicked through its pages until he found the last entry. Unsurprisingly, given the ship's port of origin, the notes were in Cyrillic, but he had enough of a working knowledge of the Russian language to make sense of it.

Starke moved in beside him as he scanned the notes that seemed to have been scribbled in a hurry. "Last entry was at 15:00 hours today. Heading was south-southwest at twelve knots. Bad weather and heavy seas reported."

The young woman glanced up at him. "No mention of engine problems?"

O'Neill shook his head.

"Maybe they never had time to log it?" she suggested, unsure.

"Maybe," he said, sounding as unconvinced as he felt.

"I'll see what else I can find."

As she moved off to survey the rest of the bridge, O'Neill turned his attention to the ship's helm controls. A glance at the engine telegraph revealed it was set to All Stop, while a check of the gyrocompass (one of the few instruments that didn't require power) showed they were facing roughly due west, drifting with the current. That was bad news, as any big waves would break against the ship's broadside, increasing their roll and, in extreme cases, the chance of capsizing.

He was just turning away when his foot touched something, causing it to roll across the floor before pinging against a command console. Reaching down, he picked up the object and held it in the beam of his flashlight. It was a 9mm brass shell casing.

"Sir, you'd better take a look," Starke said at the same moment, her voice low and urgent. "Got some blood over here."

Hurrying over, O'Neill found her crouched down on the starboard side of the room. Sure enough, the bright beam of her flashlight had picked up blood streaked across the deck. The red emergency lights had effectively camouflaged the crimson markings until she'd chanced upon them.

The young woman glanced up, her face etched with concern. "Trouble here."

Following the blood trail with his light, O'Neill could see that it led over to the hatch used to access the starboard bridge wing. The implication was clear—someone had been shot here, and their body dragged outside where it had likely been thrown overboard.

"Shit," O'Neill said, firing up his radio. "Watkins, Rodriguez, what's your sitrep?"

It was Rodriguez who replied, his transmission garbled by the storm and the layers of metal decking between the two parties. "Say . . . your last, skipper. Trans . . . breaking up."

"We may have armed hostiles aboard," he warned. "Hold position and wait for backup. Repeat, hold position."

CHAPTER 9

DEEP IN THE BOWELS of the ship, Rodriguez checked the frequency on his radio before hitting transmit again. "Skipper, negative copy on your last. Say again."

His only reply was fragments of words interspersed with garbled static.

"God damn it," he said under his breath. "The hull must be fucking up the signal."

"Quit screwing around, man," Watkins said irritably as he tried to open the bulkhead door standing in their way. "Help me with this thing."

As best they could tell, the ship's engine room lay on the other side, though the hatch had either seized up or been sealed and locked internally. Either way, a few experimental taps on the metal had confirmed that the room beyond wasn't flooded.

Shaking his head, Rodriguez turned down the volume on his now useless radio and strode forward, moving the smaller man aside none too gently.

"Jesus, get out of the way and let a real man through," he said, gripping the wheel lock holding the hatch closed, and applying his considerable strength to the task.

The powerful muscles across his shoulders and arms bunched and strained as he fought to turn the lock. The metal creaked and groaned under the pressure but refused to turn.

Finally conceding defeat, Rodriguez released his grip and backed away a step, sweating and out of breath, and staring at the door like its refusal to open was a personal slight against him. Watkins meanwhile was leaning against the wall, smirking with amusement.

"You were saying?"

Without replying, Rodriguez reached into the satchel he'd slung over his shoulder, opened it and fished out what looked like a block of plastic wrapped in green Mylar film imprinted with the logo CHARGE DEMOLITION M112. Using his knife, he sliced off a small chunk of this material and fixed it to the upper hinge on the hatch, then repeated the process for the lower hinge, pressing and molding the pliable material until it enveloped the metal structure.

"Jesus, you going Rambo on us?" Watkins asked, surprised that his comrade would resort to such extreme measures just to force open a door.

"You wanted the hatch open, right?" Rodriguez pointed out as he fixed a length of detonator cord into each piece of Composition-4 plastic explosive, then deftly wired them into a radio receiver. He'd followed this process dozens of times before, and it showed. "Better than spending an hour with a cutting torch."

"Not if it means blowing a hole in the side of this tub."

"Relax, it's just a small breaching charge." Rodriguez held up the main block of explosive. "A block like this could send this ship to the bottom in a matter of minutes, but a few ounces won't do more than blow out the hinges." He flashed a grin as he placed the block carefully back in his satchel. "Might want to step back, though."

Retreating to the far end of the passageway, both men crouched down low as Rodriguez pulled out the radio detonator unit. Checking that the unit had power, he held it up and glanced at Watkins.

"Ready to make some noise?"

For once, Watkins didn't look his usual cocky, arrogant self. "Just blow it, for Christ's sake," he said, covering his ears.

Reaching up, Rodriguez hit his radio, hoping that at least part of his message made it through the interference. "Fire in the hole."

With that, he ducked his head down and pressed the trigger.

On the bridge several decks above, O'Neill and Starke jumped as the loud concussive boom echoed through the ship, the deck trembling beneath their feet as the shock waves traveled through its steel structure.

"Jesus, what the hell was that?" Starke asked. "We hit something?"

O'Neill shook his head. He recognized the sound of a breaching charge well enough, and knew that Rodriguez carried a demolition kit amongst his gear for emergency use. What had prompted him to detonate such a charge deep within the ship was anyone's guess, but with radio contact unreliable, it was clear they'd get no answers up here.

At the same moment, his radio crackled into life. "Richards here. Skipper, I just picked up an explosion aboard. What's happening?"

"Sit tight, Richards," O'Neill instructed, already making for the stairwell. "We're going below to check it out."

*

"Jesus, you sure you've done this before?" Watkins asked irritably, shaking his head to clear the ringing in his ears.

"Quit bitching." Rodriguez pointed towards the transverse bulkhead at the end of the passageway, where the hatch was now hanging precariously from the smoking ruins of its hinges. "We're in, aren't we? Grab your tools and let's get this done."

Rising to their feet, both men advanced down the corridor, with Watkins leading the way. A good hard kick was enough to sever the last remaining chunk of twisted metal holding the hatch in place, causing it to clatter to the deck and allowing them free access to the engine space beyond.

"The generator should be around here someplace," Watkins said, his flashlight beam playing across towering pistons, pipes, and other machinery, all of it still and ominously silent. "As long as there's still fuel—"

He was cut off suddenly when a figure leaped at him from a darkened recess, a blade gleaming for a split second in the dull red light as his cry of shock and terror echoed down the empty passageway.

CHAPTER 10

O'NEILL AND STARKE WERE hurrying down the central stairwell, weapons out and ready, the clang of their boots on the steel steps echoing up through the cavernous shaft.

"What do you think happened on the bridge?" Starke asked as she vaulted nimbly down, moving with the speed and ease of youth. "A mutiny?"

"If there was a mutiny, where did the survivors go?" O'Neill replied, slightly out of breath. "The only thing I know for sure is that bloodstains and bullet casings don't make for a good day at the beach."

They'd just reached the bottom of the stairwell when they heard shouts, panicked and angry, echoing from the passageway leading aft to the engine room.

"Let him go, you sonofabitch!" came Rodriguez' distinctive low-pitched yell, accompanied by frantic shouts in Russian. "Take one more step and I blow you in half!"

Exchanging a look, both O'Neill and Starke raised their weapons and sprinted down the passageway, past the shattered and still smoking remains of the engine room bulkhead, and into the machine space beyond.

The scene that greeted them was enough to stop both Coast Guard officers in their tracks.

Rodriguez was indeed there, standing just inside the hatchway, his shotgun up at his shoulder as he tried to cover several different targets at once. Directly in front of him, maybe ten feet away, Watkins stood pinned in front of another man with a knife held at his throat, face pale and eyes wide with fear.

The man holding him hostage was partially concealed in the shadows, but O'Neill could see a brawny, tattoo-covered arm clutching the knife so tight that the veins and tendons stood out sharp beneath his inked skin. A pair of eyes glared at them beneath the red emergency lighting.

Three other men also occupied the engine room, all dressed in the grimy, oil-stained overalls of engineering staff, and varying in age from mid-twenties to late forties. All three were armed with everything from wrenches to sections of steel pipe to claw hammers. Improvised weapons snatched up in a hurry by men not expecting a fight.

The biggest of the three, clutching a huge two-foot-long pipe wrench, was trying to angle off to the left of Rodriguez, the tension in his body making it clear he intended to strike the moment his target was distracted.

"Back off!" O'Neill warned, raising his automatic and training it on the man's center mass. "Back off right now!"

Whether or not he spoke English was questionable, but a loaded 9mm SIG automatic pointed in one's face had a way of transcending most language barriers, and he halted.

"Drop your weapons!" Starke added, brandishing her own sidearm at the man holding Watkins hostage. "Let our man go. Now."

He did nothing of the sort, plainly unwilling to relinquish his only bargaining chip. One of the others, a slender young man with blond hair, snarled something at her in Russian. O'Neill's patchy knowledge of the language translated it as him greatly looking forward to urinating on her grave.

"Seb, what happened here?" O'Neill asked sharply, eyeing the four hostiles.

"They jumped us as we made entry," Rodriguez quickly explained. "Took Watkins hostage. They'd have gotten me too if I was half a second slower."

"Will someone please shoot this sonofabitch?" Watkins said through gritted teeth, keeping remarkably calm under the circumstances.

"I got nothing," Rodriguez hissed. Armed as he was with a shotgun, it was impossible for him to take down Watkins' captor without hitting his own comrade.

Starke, however, was not so encumbered. "Think I've got a shot, sir."

She was frightened. O'Neill could see the weapon trembling slightly in her hands as she stared down the sights, but she was doing a good job of hiding her fear.

No sooner had she spoken than the hostage-taker turned towards her, forcing Watkins to move in front of him and blocking her line of sight.

"Sir, what are we doing?" the young woman asked, her voice more urgent now.

At that moment, O'Neill did something that none of them had expected. He lowered his weapon.

"What the fuck are you doing?" Watkins demanded, fear and desperation showing through now. "Shoot this bastard."

But O'Neill's attention was focused on the man behind him. "You speak English," he said quietly. "I know you do. You reacted when she asked to take the shot."

The man said nothing in response, but the recognition in his eyes confirmed to O'Neill that his words were understood.

"You pretended not to understand us, because you wanted to know what we'd say to each other," he went on. "You wanted to know who we were, whether we were friends or enemies. Well, here's your answer."

With that, O'Neill holstered his weapon. There was no need for it now. What he saw wasn't some hardened terrorist ready to execute a hostage, or a murderer looking for another victim, but a desperate man pushed to violence to protect his own life and those of his crewmates.

In any case, he was quite certain Starke and Rodriguez would drop anyone who tried to make a rush at him.

"We're U.S. Coast Guard, responding to your ship's distress call. We got onboard and found the place deserted," O'Neill explained, then nodded to Watkins. "And that man is probably the only one here who can get this ship up and running, so what do you say you put down the knife? We can talk."

The man let out a breath, apparently weighing up what O'Neill had just said. "How can I trust you?" he finally asked in heavily accented but fluent English.

"The same way I just trusted you," O'Neill replied, managing to sound a lot calmer than he felt. He took a step forward, his hands up. "We're here to help."

After a few heart-stopping moments the man signaled to his comrade. The knife was finally withdrawn and his grip on Watkins slackened. Wasting no time, the mechanic tore free and hastily retreated, spinning around to face him only when he was well out of the man's reach.

"Sonofabitch!" he snarled. "Someone give me a gun so I can shoot him myself."

"Stow it, Watkins," O'Neill ordered, sensing the Russians tense at those words. "Nobody's going to open fire." He glanced at the other two members of the boarding party. "Rodriguez, Starke, lower your weapons."

Reluctantly his crew members complied, allowing O'Neill to focus on the apparent leader of the Russian group. It was the first time he'd been able to get a decent look at Watkins' former captor.

He wasn't a tall man, but he had the muscular, broad-shouldered build of one used to heavy manual labor, and the grim countenance of a man accustomed to hardship. He was likely only in his late forties, but a tough life had made its own impression on him. His features were strong and rugged, his graying hair was close-cropped, his exposed arms etched with crude tattoos that suggested he'd done prison time.

All in all, the general impression he exuded was one of brute strength and limited intellect, but his eyes told another story. There was something behind them that stood in stark contrast to his outward appearance; a keen mind that was scrutinizing O'Neill just as closely.

"You're chief engineer here?" O'Neill asked by way of introduction.

The man nodded.

"What's your name?"

A moment or two of hesitation. "Dmitry," he said at last.

"Dmitry," O'Neill repeated. "My name's Rick." Exhaling and allowing himself to relax just a little, he glanced around at the silent engine room. "Tell us what the hell happened here."

CHAPTER 11

DMITRY QUICKLY INTRODUCED HIS three comrades. The big one who had tried to lay out Rodriguez was called Oleg, the young skinny one with the blond hair was Yuri, and the third member was a brooding, shaven-headed man named Iosif. None of them seemed enthusiastic about communicating with the Coast Guard boarding party, content to let their chief engineer do the talking.

Gratefully leaving behind the claustrophobic confines of the engine room, the group made their way up to the mess hall several decks above. There O'Neill and the others listened while Dmitry, speaking in slightly broken English, did his best to relate the events leading up to their encounter.

"The engines went down about four hours ago, just as weather closed in," he began. "I do not know where problems start, but they overheat then seize up. We turn on backup generator to keep power running while we start repairs." He let out a frustrated sigh. "But we do not have tools or spare parts to make proper fix. Everything here is cheap and old and fucked up."

"Then backup generator fail too," chipped in Oleg, who only minutes earlier had harbored thoughts of taking out Rodriguez with a wrench. He'd lit up a cigarette now that they were away from the engines, and was taking deep drags on it.

Dmitry grunted in agreement. "No generator, no power. Lights go to emergency batteries only."

It wasn't hard for O'Neill to picture such an unfortunate series of events unfolding. On a ship as old and neglected as the *Ossora*, seldom-used pieces of equipment like backup generators were no doubt low on the list of maintenance priorities.

"That was when we hear the call from bridge," Dmitry went on, his flash of grim humor fading. "Fast boats coming in both sides. I go up to look around, then I hear gunshots on deck." He looked at O'Neill, as if seeking an understanding. "We were attacked."

"By who?" O'Neill asked.

Dmitry shrugged and shook his head. "I do not see them. I run back to engine room, warn my crew. Then we close and lock the hatch." It was clear from his expression that the decision to abandon the rest of the crew to their fate hadn't been an easy one, and that it still weighed heavily on his mind. "We do not hear anything more after this."

O'Neill sympathized with him, but he needed answers. "How long ago was that?"

"An hour, maybe."

No wonder the Russians had been on edge when Watkins and Rodriguez made entry. Sitting in silence for so long in the dim glow of emergency lights while the ship rocked and swayed around them, waiting for men with guns to try to force their way in, would have been enough to fray anyone's nerves.

"And you didn't try to fix the generator?"

Dmitry shook his head. "If they were still aboard, the noise would alert them."

"So you just sat there in the dark twiddling your thumbs that whole time," Watkins remarked skeptically. "Why didn't you go out and take a look?"

Dmitry turned his pale gray eyes on him. "Would you have?"

"Take it easy," O'Neill warned his surly mechanic. "We're trying to figure out what happened here, not point fingers."

"Sounds pretty much like piracy to me," Starke concluded. "Fast attack boats, an armed boarding party—"

"Bullshit," Watkins cut in. "This ain't the Indian Ocean. Who would be out in a Zodiac with a Force nine storm bearing down? And why attack an old freighter like this in the first place? Hardly seems like a gold mine."

"Good question," O'Neill conceded. For once, Watkins was on the mark. To the best of his knowledge, piracy was unheard of in this part of the world. "What were you guys hauling?"

Dmitry made a gesture of ignorance. "I work the engines, not load cargo."

"But you have a manifest onboard, right?"

He nodded.

O'Neill chewed his lip. Likely any such document would be up on the bridge or in the captain's cabin. Either way, it seemed he would need to do a little searching.

His thoughts were interrupted by the crackle of his radio. It was Richards in the MLB outside. "Skipper, come in. Over."

"Go, Richards."

"Just got word in from the *Munro*," he reported, relief brightening his voice. "I've updated her on our situation and she's on her way, making eighteen knots. Best she can manage in this weather. Should be with us in four, five hours tops."

Some good news at last, he thought. A full-sized Coast Guard cutter like the *Munro* could take the *Ossora* under tow and escort her to safe harbor for repairs. They had only to keep the ship from foundering in the rough weather until then.

No sooner had this thought crossed his mind, however, than Richards piped up again.

"There's something else. Don't want to worry you, but from out here it looks like the *Ossora* is riding pretty low in the water. Might be worth checking for flooding."

O'Neill had been afraid of that. It was unlikely the ship had been holed or damaged since they were miles from the nearest island or shoal, but with no power to run the pumps, water from the storm-lashed deck had made its way inside and started collecting in the bilges. Left unchecked it could destabilize the vessel, causing it to capsize, or simply flood the lower compartments and sink them.

Either way, something had to be done.

"Copy that, Richards. Keep an eye on it, but if it looks dangerous, cut loose and evac. Don't want you getting pulled under."

"Roger that, skip. Standing by."

Clicking off his radio, O'Neill turned to regard the small, disparate group clustered around the mess hall table. They were hardly a well oiled machine, but they were all he had to work with.

"Okay, we split up," he decided. "Watkins, take the Russian engineers down below and inspect the flooding situation, then get to work on the generator. We need power to run the bilge pumps, and we need it fast."

He held out little hope of repairing the engines with the resources at hand, since by Dmitry's own assessment they'd seized up and would likely need a complete overhaul. However, if they could generate enough power to get the pumps running, they could at least keep the vessel afloat until it could be towed into port.

"Rodriguez, get down to the cargo hold and have a look around," he went on. "If someone was willing to fight their way onboard for what this ship was carrying, I'd like to know what it is."

"I will go with you," Dmitry volunteered. "Show you the way."

O'Neill nodded. Since this ship was both large and unfamiliar, his suggestion was a sensible one. "Once you've inspected the hold, get to the engine room to assist Watkins."

"I'm on it," Rodriguez said, snatching up his shotgun.

"I've got a better idea, sir," Watkins piped up.

O'Neill turned to look at him, already quite sure he wasn't going to like what he heard. "Let's hear it."

"I say we ditch this bitch," the mechanic said. "Evac to the MLB and get the hell out of here before this storm sinks us both. We did our job, made it out here and rescued what's left of the crew. Why risk everyone's lives to save a ship that should be scrapped anyway?"

"So you just want to let it sink?" Starke challenged him. "This entire ship is a crime scene now. Plus there must be thousands of gallons of fuel in her tanks, not to mention whatever cargo she's hauling. You're talking about an environmental disaster."

Watkins glared at her. "We're Coast Guard, not EPA. Our first priority is saving lives. They're not paying us to save the planet."

"That's enough," O'Neill interrupted, beginning to lose patience with Watkins. "We're not in the habit of letting ships go down without a fight, and we're certainly not pulling out at the first sign of trouble. You have your orders, Watkins. Now, are you going to follow them, or are we going to have a real problem?"

Watkins stared at him for a long moment as the ship's frame creaked and groaned around them, straining against the waves lashing its hull. O'Neill was several inches taller than Watkins, and far heavier and stronger—three facts that were not lost on him in that moment.

"No," he said at last, deciding this was a battle best left unfought for now. "No problem, *sir*."

"Then get to it," O'Neill ordered. "Now."

Reluctantly Watkins shouldered his pack and turned to the three Russian engineers. "Okay, you three with me," he snapped. "Show me where the bilge access is on this piece of crap."

"Where do you want me?" Starke asked as the rest of the group began to break up.

O'Neill kept an eye on Watkins until he was out of the room before turning to her. "You're with me. I want a look at the ship's manifest."

CHAPTER 12

WATKINS STARED AT THE rusted, deteriorated steel hatch fixed into the deck beneath him, illuminated by the harsh glow of his flashlight. By the looks of things, it had been quite some time since this part of the ship had been inspected.

"Okay, pull it," he instructed.

Gripping the hatch cover, Oleg, the largest of the three Russian engineers, pulled upward, arms and shoulders straining as he took the weight. The hatch resisted him for a moment or two, before the rusted hinges finally gave way and the hatch swung back to reveal the darkened space below.

Straight away a noxious smell of decay and corruption filled the compartment, causing Yuri, the youngest of the engineers, to turn aside and retch. The other two had gone distinctly pale as well.

Watkins grinned at him in amusement. Being the place where seawater and all kinds of spillages ultimately pooled and collected and rarely cleaned out, the bilge was often home to some truly foul odors. It wasn't unknown for ship rats to fall in and die in the fetid water, only adding to the heady aroma.

"Smells worse than an Alabama hooker, doesn't she?" he taunted them, before approaching the open hatch and shining his flashlight inside to inspect it.

Straight away he knew they were in trouble.

"Well, that ain't good," he said, staring at the oily, scum-covered water that had risen to only a couple of feet below the level of the hatch. The movement of the ship was causing it to slosh around like a full bathtub being rocked from side to side.

If the water level continued to rise like this, it would begin to flood the lower compartments. And with no means of pumping the water out, it would only be a matter of time before the ship succumbed.

"Close it up," he said, having seen enough. He doubted the old, weakened hatch would even contain such flooding, but it was better than nothing. "We'd better get started on that generator."

O'Neill was back on the bridge, engaged in a so far fruitless search through the ship's cargo manifest, when the radio call came in from Watkins a minute or two later. "Bilge inspection complete."

"Give me some good news," O'Neill said, expecting the opposite.

"I got none for you," Watkins confirmed. "It's worse than we thought; almost up to the level of the inspection hatches. If we don't start pumping within the hour, there'll be no stopping it."

Situated high up on the ship, O'Neill could already feel the difference that hundreds of tonnes of water moving uncontrolled were making. The ship seemed to keel over a little more with each wave, and dip a little lower in the water as it passed through each trough.

"Then we'd better get that pump working, hadn't we, Mr Watkins?"

He could have sworn he heard a muffled curse over the radio net. "We're on it."

"Good. Radio when you have an update."

Watkins said nothing to that, but the sudden wash of static over the net told O'Neill he'd ceased transmitting.

"He doesn't like you," Starke warned him, standing over by the ship's wheel.

O'Neill cocked an eyebrow. "You just figured that out?"

"I mean it. Watch your back around him."

He frowned. Her warning seemed to extend beyond mere animosity from a work-shy mechanic. "Something I ought to know about?"

The young woman turned away abruptly. "It's nothing."

Clearly that was untrue. "Whatever gets said here stays between you and me, okay?"

Starke hesitated for a few moments, then with a sigh turned around to face him again. "I overheard him and Rodriguez talking on the way out here. Watkins was talking trash about you. Nothing but rumors and gossip, I guess."

O'Neill could feel his heart beating faster. "What kind of rumors?"

"Well, he . . ." If she hadn't already been surrounded by the red glow of emergency lighting, he was quite sure he would have seen a deep blush coloring her face. "He said you were involved in some kind of shady operation, that you got one of your team killed and used your connections to avoid a court-martial. That's why you ended up out here."

It had come pouring out so fast, as if she wanted to get it over with as quickly as possible, that O'Neill needed a moment or two to process it all. When he did, the familiar sinking feeling in the pit of his stomach, the sense of loss and guilt that had been lingering around him for the past few months returned with a vengeance.

"Like I say, just dumb gossip. All we've got out here," Starke said hastily, seeing his reaction. "Watkins seemed to believe it, though."

O'Neill took a step toward her. "And you? What do you believe?"

Starke opened her mouth to answer, then hesitated, seeming to think better of it.

The fraught silence was only interrupted when both of their radios sparked up, this time with Rodriguez' voice.

"Skipper, you copy?"

O'Neill was almost relieved he didn't have to hear her answer. "Go, Rodriguez."

"We just opened up Cargo Hold One."

"How's it look?" O'Ncill asked.

"Well, it's big," was Rodriguez' simple answer as he stared around at the cavernous space stretching out before him.

However, the word big scarcely seemed to do it justice. Nearly two hundred feet in length and spanning the full beam of the ship, Cargo Hold One was one of the largest internal spaces that Rodriguez had seen on any vessel. Bathed in minimal lighting, the impression created was of some great underground world into which the two tiny human explorers had ventured for the first time.

"We're starting our sweep, but there are a lot of containers in here," he warned, surveying the maze of steel boxes stretching off before him. "Could take a while. Anything on the manifest?"

"Nothing yet. Let me know what you find. O'Neill out."

Clicking off his radio, Rodriguez descended the set of steel stairs from the catwalk that encircled the upper level of the hold, with Dmitry following. The Russian however seemed less than sure-footed as the ship continued to pitch and roll, and stumbled for a moment as he lost his balance.

"Lost your sea legs?" Rodriguez asked, surprised.

"It is new to me. This is only my second trip," Dmitry explained, looking sheepish. "I fix tractor engines before I come here."

Rodriguez glanced at him, shocked. "And they made you chief engineer?"

The Russian flashed a wry grin. "Captain needs engineer, I need job. Anyway, engines are engines."

The Coast Guard seaman shook his head in disbelief. No wonder this tub had gotten into trouble so fast. Thinking it best not to question him further, Rodriguez shone his light on the first of many steel shipping containers laid out along both sides of the room. This was a forty-foot unit; one of the largest of its kind that could reasonably fit into most shipping holds.

He moved closer to inspect it, and found it locked and secured with heavy chains and padlocks. Reaching out, he held up the lock, looking for any signs of tampering.

"Be careful," Dmitry warned him.

Rodriguez frowned. "Something I ought to know, chief?"

"Lock is not the only safety measure," the engineer explained. "Many shipping contractors in Russia booby-trap containers. Stop people fucking with their cargo."

"So you're saying this thing could blow up in my face?"

Dmitry shrugged. "Maybe. You want to test it, be my guest. I will stand back."

"Fuck that," Rodriguez decided, allowing the lock to fall back into place with a metallic clang.

A visual inspection of another dozen or so units yielded up nothing of note. All of them looked sound and untouched as far as he could tell, and he suspected it would be a similar story with the others. Certainly none of their doors appeared to be open, and he doubted pirates would take the time to carefully lock up after themselves if they'd come down here to steal something.

"Ever get the feeling this is a wild goose chase?" he asked, his voice echoing down the big compartment.

"No geese here, my friend," Dmitry replied, clearly misunderstanding.

"Yup, that about covers it." Rodriguez fired up his radio again. "Skipper, come in."

"Yeah, Rodriguez?"

"I'm not seeing anything unusual down here. Whatever these pirates were after, I don't think it was in the cargo hold."

There was a pause. "Copy that. Get yourselves to the engine room and help Watkins with the generator."

"With pleasure." Rodriguez was just turning toward Dmitry when he paused, alerted by an unusual sound.

A thumping noise, soft and muted, coming from nearby.

"You hear that?" he asked.

The Russian stopped, looking perplexed. "What?"

"Shh!" Rodriguez stood still, straining to hear over the creak and groans of the old ship riding out the storm.

There! He heard it again, a soft thump. Something hitting a metal surface.

"Maybe something hit the hull?" Dmitry suggested.

Rodriguez shook his head. "No way, it's inside the compartment." His flashlight beam played across the steel boxes lined up around them. "It's coming from one of the containers."

Slowly retracing his steps as quietly as possible, he listened intently until he heard it again, closer now. His instincts told him it was coming from the next container along—Number 29.

"Maybe cargo shift inside it," Dmitry said.

Frowning, Rodriguez reached out and thumped the side of the container twice with his fist. Moments later, the container resounded with the same two thumps, coming from inside.

"Sonofabitch," he gasped, eyes opening wide in shock. "There's someone—"

He was just turning toward his Russian counterpart when something slammed hard into the side of his head. There was an explosion of pain and white light, followed by growing darkness as his legs gave way beneath him and he collapsed to the deck.

The Russian looked down on the unconscious man without emotion, then tossed aside the wrench he'd used against Rodriguez and reached for the radio concealed in his overalls.

He spoke a single terse command in Russian. "It's time."

CHAPTER 13

"WHAT THE FUCK?" WATKINS said, having found the source of the generator problem but refusing to believe it was something so simple. "Tell me you guys remembered to open the coolant feeds when you turned this thing on?"

The generator was equipped with a computerized management system. Without fresh water cycling through to cool it down, it had recorded a dangerous temperature spike and shut itself off to prevent damage. Anyone with half a brain could have seen that.

The Russian engineering team looked away uncomfortably, apparently having no idea what he was talking about. And somehow he doubted it was because of language differences.

"Jesus, who did you screw to get this job anyway?" he mumbled, opening the fresh water valve and clambering out from beneath the unit. He glanced at the young guy with the short blond hair who was standing by the generator control panel. "Okay, fire it up, erm . . . Yuri," he said, struggling to remember his name. "If you can manage that, I mean."

Shooting him an irritated look, Yuri turned the security key, then hit the green start-up button. The unit turned over once, then twice, caught on a little and seemed to fade out. Watkins held his breath, then suddenly the generator rumbled into life as fuel began to flow into its combustion chamber.

Almost immediately the mains lights around them flickered on, replacing the dull red glow of emergency lighting, and ventilation machinery hummed back into activity as the ship returned to life. It was a relief to feel fresh air circulating again.

"There, that wasn't so hard, was it?" Watkins grinned, only to be met with a wall of disapproving frowns, as if they resented him doing what they plainly couldn't. "You're welcome, by the way."

Feeling pleased with himself, Watkins made for the nearest wall-mounted intercom and hit the button for the bridge. Restoring power had also rebooted the ship's internal communications system.

"Bridge, this is your friendly engine room staff calling," he began sarcastically. "Looks like we're back in business."

"Good job, Watkins," O'Neill said, paying him a rare compliment. "How soon can we start pumping water out?"

"Right now. She should be ready to go, unless these guys have somehow screwed up the bilge pumps too."

"All right. Fire it up."

"Copy that." He turned away from the intercom to bark some orders at the engineering crew—only to freeze at the sight of three automatics trained on him. "What the hell is this?"

"Get down on knees," the big one, Oleg, commanded.

Watkins hesitated less than a second before suddenly turning and making a run for the intercom. Oleg was faster: grabbing Watkins before he could reach the unit, he hurled him across the room like a rag doll. He landed hard against a set of coolant pipes fixed against the hull, bruising his back and knocking the breath from his lungs.

Springing forward again on instinct, he tried to launch himself at the far larger and stronger opponent but a pair of arms seized him from behind. A kick to the back of his knee dropped him to the deck, and he looked up just as Oleg swung the pistol down on his head.

CHAPTER 14

O'NEILL WAS ON THE bridge, where status boards and navigation consoles were now flickering back into action. As they did so, various alarms began to sound, long-neglected systems performing automatic status checks and reporting on the problems that had arisen while the power was off, chief amongst which were the bilge flooding alarms.

"That doesn't sound good," Starke observed.

O'Neill glanced at her. "Ever known an alarm that did?"

Disabling the loud, urgent alarm tone, O'Neill scanned the unfamiliar controls until he found the enabling switches for the emergency bilge pump, and turned them on. Time would tell whether it was enough to counteract the flooding, but at the very least, it might buy them time until the *Munro* arrived with more personnel and equipment.

Crossing to the intercom station, he found the button for the engine room and hit it. "Watkins, come in," he said, and waited for a response.

When one wasn't forthcoming, he repeated: "Watkins, any engineering personnel, respond." Still there was nothing, and an attempt to raise him via his walkie-talkie yielded similar results.

"Comms could be on the fritz again," Starke suggested.

"Maybe," he agreed, though he was unable to quell the uneasy feeling that had stirred in the pit of his stomach. Hesitating a moment, he nodded as if to himself and turned to his subordinate. "I'm going down there to take a look, find out what's what. Stay here and keep an eye on things."

"Be careful, skipper," the young woman said just as he was leaving.

O'Neill lingered for a moment in the doorway, not sure what to say to her, before heading below, leaving Starke alone on the bridge.

In the Motor Life Boat outside, Wyatt Richards grimaced as the small Coast Guard vessel bumped against the unyielding hull of the *Ossora*, propelled by another big wave that had come crashing in. He was by now thoroughly sick of enduring these stormy conditions, and eager to cast off.

The MLB was designed to right itself automatically in the event of being capsized, but it was by its nature made of lightweight materials that could endure only so much punishment. If hit hard enough, it would break apart like driftwood against the much larger cargo vessel.

That was not a comforting thought.

Spotting movement above, he glanced up just as a figure swung over the deck railing and descended quickly by a rope harness they'd rigged up. He couldn't make out much in the spray and darkness, but he did recognize the distinctive Coast Guard wet-weather gear.

Hope surged through him. Perhaps O'Neill had ordered an evacuation. Or maybe he was to head back to base rather than risk the MLB in such dangerous conditions. Either way, it was better than sitting alone on the vessel's cramped bridge, being thrown around like a toy.

Waiting until the boarding party member had descended to deck level, Richards zipped up his jacket, yanked open the hatch and stepped out to greet them.

"Hey, what's going on up there?" he asked, having to yell to be heard over the howling wind.

Suddenly the hood slipped back, revealing a face that didn't belong to any of his teammates.

"Oh, shit!" Richards gasped, immediately going for his sidearm.

He never got the chance to draw his weapon. Richards jumped at the sudden flare of a muzzle, and the deafening crack that echoed across the empty sea. He staggered back, blood painting his rain-soaked jacket, only for a second shot to ring out moments later.

He fell, collapsing on the rocking deck with his own blood pooling around him, still wearing an expression of blank, uncomprehending shock.

Satisfied that his task was complete, Dmitry hit his radio transmitter. "It's done. Secure the bridge. Hurry."

CHAPTER 15

O'NEILL STOPPED IN HIS tracks, alerted by the distinct crack of a gunshot outside, his heart beating wildly as the realization began to dawn on him that nothing aboard this ship was what it seemed.

"Richards, give me a sitrep," he demanded.

Nothing but static greeted him.

"Richards, sound off!"

Abandoning his plan to descend to the engine room, O'Neill drew his SIG automatic and sprinted down the narrow companionway, turning right then throwing open the outside hatch to exit onto the deck.

He emerged into howling winds and freezing rain that immediately stung his exposed flesh, the chill northerly wind adding to the falling temperatures. None of these things concerned him at that moment, however. Leaning out over the rail, he was able to make out the distinctive grey and red hull of the MLB in the churning waters below.

And he was just in time to see a lifeless body in Coast Guard gear shoved roughly overboard into the swell, leaving behind a red stain on the deck where he'd been lying.

"Oh, Christ," he gasped in horror, realizing that Richards had just been murdered. For all he knew, Rodriguez and Watkins could be dead too.

It had all been a lie, he knew now. Dmitry and the rest of his "engineering" team were in fact the very men responsible for the deaths of the *Ossora*'s crew. He had no idea who they really were or what their objective in all this had been, but he did know one thing—he'd walked right into their trap. And now at least one of his crew was dead.

Such had been his focus on the terrible scene playing out below, he hadn't immediately noticed a second man on the deck about fifty feet away, standing at the portside railing. It was only when the man let out a warning cry that O'Neill's gaze turned towards him.

It was Iosif, the bald dome of his head now slick with rainwater and gleaming faintly in the glare of the newly reactivated deck lights. But O'Neill's focus was less on the man than the weapon he was now swinging around to bear on him.

O'Neill reacted on instinct, throwing himself aside just as the first burst of automatic gunfire rang out. Some of the heavy-caliber slugs flattened against the ship's superstructure, and another shattered the nearby viewing port, but others found their way in through the open hatch, ricocheting wildly around in the confined space like angry hornets. Pinned down, O'Neill could do little more than press himself against the deck and hope.

The thunderous show of firepower lasted only a couple of terrible moments before the shooter realized he'd failed to score a kill and ceased fire to reload. Using the momentarily lull in firing, O'Neill seized the outer hatch and swung it closed with a resounding clang. No sooner had it locked in place than several fist-sized dents appeared in the metalwork from the next flurry of gunfire, and he winced as a sliver of steel spalled off the hatch frame to slice the skin across his cheek.

O'Neill backed away several paces to where an emergency fire axe was fixed to the wall, inside a protective glass case. Shattering the case with his elbow, he wrenched the axe out of its holder and jammed it into the hatch locking mechanism. He didn't imagine his makeshift barricade would last long, but hopefully it would delay his pursuer long enough to cover his escape.

Sprinting back along the corridor toward the stairwell, he keyed his radio. "Starke, anyone else who's receiving, get the hell out and take cover! The Russians are hostiles! I say again, take—"

As he rounded the corner a dark figure leaped at him from the stairwell to his right, a huge bulky mass of muscle and fury. It was Oleg.

O'Neill whirled right and brought the SIG automatic into the firing position, finger tightening on the trigger, but Oleg's arm swept up and knocked it from his grasp. The weapon flew through the air to land several yards away, skittering across the deck before coming to rest against a water pipe running upward between decks.

Seeing Oleg draw back his fist to take a swing at him, O'Neill dodged aside and struck out, feeling his fist connect hard with the man's bearded jaw. The hit barely seemed to bother his opponent, and a moment later O'Neill grunted in pain as Oleg landed a solid blow to the side of his head, followed a second later by a right hook that left his ears ringing.

O'Neill threw another punch in desperation, but his opponent caught his arm and yanked him forward. Caught off balance, he looked up in time to see Oleg lean back and head-butt him. It was a perfect strike, and O'Neill groaned as white light flashed before his eyes.

Dazed, he staggered back as Oleg launched himself forward, tackling O'Neill around the waist like a quarterback and slamming him into the wall with bruising force. Oleg must have weighed a good two hundred and thirty pounds, and every one of them was now directed at O'Neill. The steel wall shuddered under the powerful impact.

Oleg snarled something in Russian before drawing himself back and driving his shoulder into O'Neill's stomach again.

O'Neill had fought guys bigger and stronger than himself before. The key was to use their size against them, keep your distance, capitalize on their lack of agility to wear them down. That was the theory, at least. In reality, it was now a slugging match, pure and simple.

He raised his elbow up and slammed it into Oleg's back, right between the shoulder blades. The big man grunted, and O'Neill struck again with all the force he could summon.

Oleg pulled back to throw another punch that would finish his opponent off. But just as he swung, O'Neill ducked to avoid the blow. The wall shuddered again as Oleg's fist slammed into the metal shell with bone-breaking force.

As the Russian stood clutching his injured hand, O'Neill seized him by the shoulder and gave him a knee to the chest that knocked the air from his lungs, followed by two vicious right hooks to the face. His opponent staggered back, giving O'Neill the opening he needed.

Throwing himself to the ground, he snatched up the fallen SIG just as the Russian recovered and came at him again.

"Don't!" O'Neill snarled, flicking the safety catch off.

Oleg stopped in his tracks, staring down the barrel of the weapon almost in confusion, as if he couldn't work out why his opponent hadn't fired.

O'Neill coughed, tasting blood in his mouth. He knew he'd regret this little tussle when he woke up tomorrow morning, assuming he lived that long, but adrenaline was doing a good job of suppressing the pain for now.

"Get down on the ground," he ordered.

Oleg didn't move, though his eyes had flicked from the weapon to the man holding it. It was clear that he sensed a weakness in his adversary; a weakness that he could exploit.

"Do it," Oleg growled, spitting bloody phlegm on the deck. "You afraid, American?"

O'Neill's finger tightened on the trigger, the weapon trembling in his hands as he struggled to act. Oleg took a step towards him, testing his resolve.

"Get the fuck down!" O'Neill shouted, taking a step back.

The Russian smiled, knowing he had his enemy on the back foot. O'Neill was in his mind a coward, too afraid to pull the trigger. He took another step forward, gathering himself to charge at his opponent.

However, before Oleg had a chance to act, the hatch on the port side flew open, helped by a burst of close-range automatic gunfire, and two armed men rushed into the corridor.

Just for a moment, O'Neill's eyes met Dmitry's, and he saw a fleeting look of triumph and malicious joy as the Russian raised his weapon.

Oleg dropped to the deck just as Dmitry and Iosif opened fire simultaneously, spraying the far end of the corridor with 7.62mm projectiles.

O'Neill dived around the corner and felt something zip past his arm, tearing through his jacket and leaving behind a sharp, stinging sensation where it passed close to the skin. Getting to his feet, he went for the starboard access hatch, yanked the locking mechanism over and kicked it open, emerging into the darkness and freezing wind outside.

There was nowhere left to run. Fifty yards of open deck stretched out in front of him—an easy killing field for two men armed with AK assault rifles. He could try to make a stand in the hatchway, but his enemies had the numbers and the firepower. Sooner or later they would outflank him, and he couldn't fend off two groups at the same time.

To stand and fight would be suicidal.

As he heard heavy footsteps approaching fast down the corridor, O'Neill turned his eyes towards the starboard railing and the dark churning waters below. The sea temperature had to be close to freezing. A man couldn't survive more than a few minutes in it.

But what choice was there?

O'Neill sprinted over to the edge and vaulted up over the railing.

CHAPTER 16

O'NEILL BROKE THE SURFACE with an agonized gasp as the freezing water clawed at him; a million tiny slivers of ice driven into every inch of his body. The pain and shock of the impact had been enough to take his breath away, but the onslaught of cold was far worse.

He looked up at the black, rust-streaked hull of the *Ossora* rising high and indomitable above him, like the flanks of some unclimbable mountain.

Focusing his mind as best he could, he tried to remember the layout of the ship. There had been an access ladder fixed to the hull on the port side, roughly midway along the main deck. Assuming the ship was constructed with any form of logic, there should be a corresponding ladder on the starboard side.

If there wasn't, he could abandon any hope of survival.

Kicking and pulling himself along the hull with desperate strength, he soon found that he was moving with the strong current and wave action, which aided his efforts but put him in constant danger of being dashed against the unyielding steel walls. It also meant he'd need to get a good grip of the ladder first time, if there even was one, or risk being swept away by the waves.

Even with the sea drawing him onward, it seemed to take a lifetime to move along the hull, and he soon began to lose feeling in his hands and feet. That was how it started, he knew. Pretty soon his core temperature would start to drop too, his movements would grow sluggish and uncoordinated, his vision would blur and his decision-making would be impaired. Without even being aware of it, his body and mind would start to shut down as the cold overwhelmed them.

This thought lent fresh impetus to his efforts, and he kicked with renewed vigor, the hull plates sliding by faster now.

He was just beginning to feel a moment of hope when suddenly he was hit by something from above, the force of it driving him right under the surface. Freezing seawater filled his lungs, and panic gripped him as he fought and kicked frantically.

He finally emerged coughing and spluttering, desperately trying to draw breath. Looking up, he caught a glimpse of a torrent of water cascading from the side of the ship, and felt a surge of anger at himself. He'd swum right under the discharge from the bilge pumps, nearly drowning in the process.

But there was no time to berate himself further, because he'd spotted something else on the hull: a set of steel rungs ascending up to deck level. Rallying what remained of his strength, O'Neill fought his way towards them, trying to time his approach with the motion of the waves.

Almost there. He tensed and flexed his fingers, trying to regain some sensation and prepare himself for what was coming.

Another swell lifted him upward just as he came within range. The hull rushed suddenly to meet him, and he slammed into it with bruising force.

Groping blindly, he felt his numb fingers touch against something, and he seized on it. He gripped the lowest rung of the ladder and managed to hook his arm around it just as the wave receded below, leaving him hanging in mid-air.

He slipped a little, his tenuous hold threatening to fail, only for the water to rise up and envelop him once more. Realizing this could be his last chance, he used the force of the upswell to reach for a higher rung.

Climb! His mind screamed at him to climb, before his salvation was swept away.

He swung his legs onto the lowest rung of the ladder, got purchase, and began his slow, tortuous ascent, one rung at a time. A lifetime ago, when he'd first boarded the *Ossora,* the climb had seemed difficult and tiresome by itself. This time however, it was a living nightmare. Wind and spray and pellets of snow buffeted his already weakened and cold-racked body as he clawed his way upward, digging deep into whatever reserves of strength remained to him.

He was certain the metal rungs would have frozen his skin if he could still feel his hands, which barely retained enough function to grip the ladder. Twice his feet slipped away from him, threatening to plunge him back into the dark depths below, and twice he somehow managed to cling grimly on, gather his wits and continue.

He no longer looked up or down to chart his progress. It felt like he'd been climbing forever, and in some part of his mind he'd given up on ever reaching the top. It was an unattainable goal, he knew now;

just something to be glimpsed in the distance but never reached. All that mattered was the next rung, and the next, and the one after that.

Then the rungs vanished, and instead of the black, pitted hull plates right before his eyes, he saw instead an expanse of flat deck. He felt like a man wandering the desert for days who had just laid eyes on a shimmering oasis.

Almost refusing to believe it, he heaved himself up over the lip of metal, then promptly collapsed on the deck and curled up into a fetal position. Somehow he'd made it, but he was deathly tired. And it felt so good to rest.

Just for a few moments.

No! He couldn't allow himself to rest now. He might have been out of the sea, but he was still soaked and freezing. It would be so easy to fall asleep and die of exposure right there on the deck.

Heaving himself up, he rose to his feet on shaky legs, took cover behind the solid bulk of a mooring capstan and looked around, trying hard to stay focused. As he'd surmised, the access ladder had brought him on deck about midway along the ship's hull. Behind stood the towering white block of the ship's superstructure, brightly illuminated now, while up ahead beyond the cargo hatches lay the forecastle; the bow of the ship.

The choice now was which direction to take.

Returning to the bridge and crew areas would likely yield up dry clothes and a chance to get warm, but there were four armed men prowling the area to contend with. Barely able to walk, he was in no condition to take on anyone.

That left the forecastle, which was more of a machine space than an accommodation area. But at least it would give him a chance to escape the relentless wind and rain.

Making his decision, he turned and hurried towards it, keeping as low as possible to avoid being seen. His breath was coming in shallow gasps, his heart hammering and his steps leaden as he approached the raised deck at the bow of the ship.

A pair of access hatches, one on each side, were his only way in. Making for the starboard one, he tried the lock, relieved to find it hadn't been barred from inside, and shoved it open, before stumbling inside and heaving it closed.

In the dimly lit machine space beyond, O'Neill let out a shuddering breath and slumped back against the wall, freezing and exhausted. He'd come as far as he could for now, and could go no farther.

That was when he heard it. The unmistakable click of a hammer being drawn back on a weapon.

"Don't move," a voice warned him.

O'Neill looked up as a figure emerged from the shadows on the other side of the compartment.

CHAPTER 17

AFTER HEARING THE HEAVY splash of the Coast Guard officer impacting the water thirty feet below, Dmitry knew that if the fall hadn't killed him, the sea certainly would.

Now up on the bridge, Dmitry stared out at the storm-tossed sea, his expression as dark as the churning waves that surrounded them as he held the satellite phone to his ear, waiting for it to be answered.

Somewhere out there, beyond the horizon, an armed Coast Guard cutter was bearing down on them at flank speed. He'd listened in on their radio transmissions from the MLB below, shortly before destroying the long-range radio. If their reports were accurate, they would be here in under three hours.

He fully intended to be gone before they arrived. But to make that happen, and forestall further pursuit, he had much work to do in a short space of time.

Finally the call connected, and a breathless, raspy voice answered. "You're late."

Dmitry could feel a chill run through him at the brisk, reproachful greeting. His employer was not a man one kept waiting. "It couldn't be helped. We've had some problems here."

"What kind of problems?"

"Nothing we can't handle, but we may have to bring the cargo ashore sooner than expected," Dmitry explained. "I'd appreciate if you could have transport standing by."

Silence greeted him for a moment or two. "I've invested a lot in this venture, and in you, Dmitry. I'd hate to think I'd made a bad choice."

Dmitry managed to keep his voice calmer than he felt when he spoke again. "We will deliver the cargo as promised. You have my word on that."

"I hope so, for your sake."

The brief, terse exchange completed, he hung up.

"The two hostages are secured in the engine room," Oleg reported, having stood in silence while Dmitry conducted his call. "Yuri is guarding them."

Turning his gaze away from the turbulent conditions outside, Dmitry regarded his subordinate. One side of his face was cut and bruised from his earlier clash with O'Neill, but he seemed otherwise unharmed. The man was as tough as a bar of iron, if only marginally smarter.

"And the woman?" Dmitry asked. Oleg had originally been tasked with ascending to the bridge, and killing or capturing O'Neill and the young woman Starke, but he'd instead become embroiled in a fight with the leader of the Coast Guard boarding party.

The big man glanced away. "We're still looking for her."

"Then she's a threat," Dmitry concluded. A marginal threat to be sure, and unlikely to seriously challenge four armed men, but it was a threat he could do without. He had enough problems to deal with already.

"I'll take care of it," Oleg said, guessing his thoughts. Snatching up his AKS-74, he turned to leave the bridge.

"No," Dmitry commanded him. Oleg had already proven himself unreliable in combat. "I have other work for you. Get to the Coast Guard vessel and keep watch over it."

The big man hesitated, then reluctantly nodded and turned to leave. He knew better than to argue with Dmitry.

As Oleg left, Dmitry turned his attention to the other man standing by on the bridge. Iosif, the cold and remorseless killer from St Petersburg who had so efficiently dispatched the *Ossora*'s crew.

"Take this," Dmitry said, tossing him the canvas satchel that had once been carried by Rodriguez. "You know what to do. Engine room and cargo holds, and make sure the internal hatches are open."

Oleg nodded. "Consider it done."

"And when you are finished," Dmitry added, "hunt that bitch down and kill her."

The Russian smiled, turning to leave without saying another word.

CHAPTER 18

O'NEILL STARED IN DISBELIEF as the figure that emerged from the shadows suddenly resolved itself into a young, dark-haired woman dressed in Coast Guard gear. His heart surged at the realization that she was alive.

"Kate," O'Neill said, his voice a ragged, pained rasp as he managed to rise to his feet and take a step towards her.

"Rick! Jesus, I thought you were one of them," Starke exclaimed, lowering her gun and striding forward to meet him.

She was just in time. His vision growing hazy, O'Neill's head swam, and he stumbled and almost fell, saved only when Starke caught him and gently lowered him to the deck.

"It's all right. You're okay," she said, shocked by the pale, shivering man kneeling before her. "What happened to you?"

"Had to take a swim," he replied, managing a weak smile as he hugged his arms close to his chest, trying to generate a little warmth.

Her eyes opened wider. "Christ, you're freezing!"

Without a moment's hesitation, she unzipped her jacket and pulled it off.

O'Neill tried to stop her, but he lacked the strength or the coordination to make much of an effort. "No, you don't have to—"

"Bullshit I don't. You'll freeze to death if you don't get some dry clothes on," she cut in firmly, removing his coat and inadvertently exposing a bloody wound along his upper right arm—torn fabric and torn flesh beneath. "God damn it, you're hit. Anything else you want to tell me?"

O'Neill glanced down, surprised by what he saw. The bullet that had whizzed by as he dived around that corner must have come a little closer than he'd thought. Between the adrenaline rush of his escape and the numbing effects of the frigid water, he'd barely felt a thing.

"It's not bad," he said, not certain if that was true. At least the bleeding didn't seem serious, and as his recent climb proved, he still had use of the arm.

Starke thought about it for a moment, but decided raising his body temperature was higher priority than treating a flesh wound and set about forcing his arms into her own jacket. It was rather too small for his large frame, but it was dry and still warm. Soon enough he began to feel the effects, helped by her wrapping her arms around him to share body heat.

The shivering settled down, and his thoughts became clearer. He was still soaking wet and cold, but hypothermia was less of a threat for now.

"How . . . how did you . . . " he began.

"Get away?" she finished for him. "When I heard gunshots, I looked out from the bridge and saw shooting on the portside deck, so I bailed out through the outside stairs on the starboard side. I guess they didn't see me, because I made it this far. Figured this was the last place they'd come looking."

"Why didn't you radio me?" he asked.

"For all I knew, they could be listening in. If I gave away my position they'd come looking for me." She sighed, looking ashamed. "Not exactly heroic."

O'Neill nodded, impressed that she'd had the presence of mind to take such a precaution. "You did the right thing."

He didn't expect such reassurance to cut much ice with her, and he was right. "Rick, tell me what's going on," she implored him. "Who the hell are these people?"

O'Neill swallowed hard. "I don't know, but they killed the *Ossora*'s crew and tried to do the same to us." His hands clenched into fists as he thought about the body being dumped unceremoniously into the water. "Wyatt's dead."

Starke's mouth opened wide in shock. "You're sure?"

He nodded grimly. "Saw it with my own eyes."

The young woman closed her eyes for a moment, silently mourning the loss of one of their comrades. "What about Watkins and Rodriguez?"

"I don't know," he admitted. "But I know they weren't answering their comms."

Starke let out a defeated sigh, leaning back against the wall. "So we're all that's left."

"For now," he conceded. Reaching out, he laid a hand on her shoulder and stared into her eyes. "But we're not done yet."

"But what can we do?" she asked.

"The *Munro*'s on her way. We only need to keep them busy until then." He thought about it for a moment. "We know this ship isn't getting away under her own power, and the lifeboats are too slow to get anywhere in this weather. That leaves the MLB. They must be planning to escape in it."

"So we steal it back from them," Starke concluded.

O'Neill looked at her. "*We* don't do anything. I'll take care of it."

The young woman frowned. "So what am I supposed to do?"

"Stay here. Stay safe."

"You really think I'm going to let you go out there alone?"

"You don't need to *let* me do anything," he said, rising to his feet with difficulty. "I'm still your CO, and I'm ordering you to stay here."

"If this is some chivalrous crap—"

"It's not about that!" he snapped, immediately regretting it. Letting out a breath, he forced himself to calm down. "I just . . . I don't want another death on my conscience."

Starke too rose to her feet. "That's a line of thought you need to shut down. There's nothing you could have done for Richards, and you know it." Seeing the haunted look in his eyes, she hesitated, sensing there was something more he wasn't telling her. "But this isn't just about Richards, is it? This is something else."

"You don't want to know," he said evasively.

"It's the same reason you didn't pull the trigger in that engine room when Dmitry took Watkins hostage," she pressed on. "The same reason you ended up out here in the first place. What the hell happened to you, Rick?"

O'Neill sighed and looked down. He'd come close to telling her earlier, back at Attu Station, but he'd held off. Afraid of what her reaction would be. Afraid of what she'd think.

But he was tired of hiding from the truth.

"Those rumors you heard about me," he said at last, his voice quiet and pensive. "They're true. I did get a man killed."

Starke said nothing to this. Instead she waited, giving him the time he needed.

"I was part of the MSRT," he went on.

"The armed response teams?"

O'Neill nodded grimly. Maritime Security Response Teams were an elite amongst the Coast Guard, deployed in situations where armed resistance was almost guaranteed.

"We'd boarded a freighter in the Gulf of Mexico that we'd been told was shipping cocaine in from South America. We fast-roped in from a chopper and secured the deck, then split up to search the ship. That was when it happened." O'Neill took a breath. "Pete Clarke, a guy I'd served with nearly five years. We went through MSRT selection together. One of the smugglers managed to ambush him and put a gun to his head, used him as a human shield. He was demanding that we let him go or he'd pull the trigger. I had the shot, and I wasn't about to let that sonofabitch get away with taking my friend hostage. So I took it. No hesitation; I just fired."

O'Neill closed his eyes as that terrible moment played out in his mind once again.

"I can't rightly say what happened, no matter how many times I see it in my head. Maybe he moved at the wrong moment, maybe the deck shifted beneath us. But I missed, hit Pete just above the left eye. And that was it for him. He died in surgery an hour or so later." He opened his eyes again and looked at Starke, feeling oddly relieved to have shared the truth with someone. "Watkins was wrong about one thing, though. I didn't use any connections to avoid a court-martial. I asked for one, but they refused, said it was an accident, that making it all public would drag everyone through the mud. I was finished there, couldn't bring myself to draw a weapon on anyone again. So I left, gave up my position in the response teams and requested a transfer to the most remote posting they could give me. And here I am."

The young woman was silent for a moment or two, clearly stunned by what she'd heard. "I didn't know . . ."

"Now you do. The guy who led you out here is a fucking fraud who isn't fit for his command, Kate." He snorted with grim humor. "I was typing up my resignation letter when you came into my office. A day later and I wouldn't even be here."

"But you *are* here," she said, reaching out and touching his arm. "So am I. Whatever you did in the past . . . it doesn't matter anymore. What matters is what we do now, tonight. We can still stop Dmitry and the others getting away with this, but we have to work together."

He shook his head. "I told you I don't want another death on my conscience."

"And I told you I'm going, whether you order me or not." For the first time since their reunion, she flashed a faint, defiant smile. "You can court-martial me later if you want, *sir*."

O'Neill looked at her for a long moment, saying nothing.

CHAPTER 19

CHECKING FOR THE THIRD time that it wasn't hooked up to a power source, Iosif inserted the length of detonator cord into the lump of gray-white material he'd duct taped against the ship's hull. A veteran of the Russian army, he knew all too well the risks associated with rigging explosives. The potential for fatal fuck-ups was never far away.

In this case however, he needn't have worried. The Composition-4 demolition charge pilfered from the Coast Guard boarding party was top grade military explosive, extremely stable and as pliable as Play-Doh. It could be shaped into virtually any form one desired.

With this done, the last step was to hook the det cord up to the remote detonator unit. The charge was now armed and ready to be blown. A similar explosive device had been set up on the other side of the vast cargo hold, as well as two more in the engine room. They needed to blow both sides of the ship simultaneously if it was to sink properly, otherwise they risked capsizing it and trapping air pockets inside that could keep it afloat for hours.

He was just packing away the tools he'd used for his work, when a noise at the far end of the hold caught his attention. The metallic ping of a dropped bolt or screw accidentally kicked. The soft shuffling of feet on the steel deck.

Gently picking up his AKS assault rifle to avoid scraping the barrel on the deck, Iosif rose slowly to his feet and raised the weapon to his shoulder, advancing slowly down the hold while keeping to the shadows.

He'd fought many a desperate battle in the ruins of Chechnya and knew how to use cover and concealment to his advantage, as well as how to move silently. With light levels at a minimum, Iosif strained to hear instead.

There! Movement, thirty yards away, starboard side. It was coming towards him.

Creeping forward until he was positioned between two shipping containers, he crouched down and gently flicked the safety catch off, eyes scanning the gloom. He was like a hunter on a game trail, waiting for his prey to come to him.

It didn't take long.

Thirty seconds later, a figure finally moved into view. A woman for sure, judging by the small frame, crouched down low and moving warily, trying to stay hidden. Completely unaware that he already had the drop on her.

Then she spotted him. The woman froze. He heard a sharp intake of breath, and saw her starting to tremble. She was frightened, as well she should be. She was going to die in this place.

"Do not move," Iosif said, emerging from his hiding place with the weapon up at his shoulder. From this range, he simply couldn't miss.

The woman was pale, her dark hair wet and tangled, but in ordinary life he imagined she was quite attractive, still in the bloom of youth. Shame, he thought as his finger tightened on the trigger. The world always missed a pretty girl.

He expected to see fear in her eyes as his intention became clear, but strangely there was no sign of it in this woman. Either she was braver than most of the men he'd killed in his lifetime, or too stupid to realize this was it for her.

"Drop it," another voice growled in his ear.

Instinctively Iosif started to turn towards it, but the cold barrel of a weapon pressed against the side of his head was enough to dissuade him.

"I said drop the gun," the voice repeated. "Don't make me ask again."

Recognizing that his position was hopeless, Iosif lowered the weapon. Straight away Starke moved forward and snatched it from his grip before turning it on him.

"Good timing," she remarked.

It was a trap, he knew. The woman had been a decoy to lure him out. Somehow O'Neill had survived his plunge into the freezing sea. The bastard was resilient if nothing else.

Iosif glanced over at O'Neill, who still had the pistol at his head. "This will make no difference," he spat. "You have no—"

He was silenced when O'Neill swung the pistol around against his head, knocking him unconscious.

CHAPTER 20

IOSIF AWOKE A SHORT time later. He'd been moved to a different part of the ship; one that he didn't recognize. However, heavy machinery and the thick links of anchor chains stretching across the room told him he was somewhere in the bow. His hands were bound to one of these chains by plastic cable ties.

Starke and O'Neill were standing in front of him.

"Good, you're awake," O'Neill said, staring him hard in the eye. "We're short on time, so I want some answers fast. Where are the rest of my team?"

"Fuck you," Iosif spat.

"Last chance," O'Neill warned.

Iosif glared at him. "You won't kill me. You are coward."

At this, the Coast Guard officer smiled. "You're right, I won't." He nodded to the young woman at his side. "But she will."

Without saying anything further, Starke turned towards the heavy anchor windlass around which the chains were wrapped, gripped the brake release handle and pulled it downward.

Immediately Iosif was jerked away from them, pulled by the inexorable weight of tonnes of steel anchor and chain being lowered into the sea. He was being pulled towards the anchor well at the far end of the room.

"What are you doing?" he yelled. "Stop!"

But the look on the young woman's face made it clear she had no intention of stopping.

"What do you think, Rick? Will he fit through?"

O'Neill shook his head. "Nah, he's too fat," he said, forced to speak louder to be heard over the clanking chains. "I'm guessing the anchor well will tear him up."

"Stop this!" Iosif shouted, yanking and straining against his bonds as the chain pulled him closer and closer to the opening. It was a futile effort. He knew from experience that they were virtually unbreakable. "You can't!"

"Only one way this is going to stop, Iosif," O'Neill warned him. "Feel like talking yet?"

His hands were almost at the anchor well now. It was clear he'd never fit through such a gap, and would likely see his arms ripped off by the force of the descending chain.

"All right!" he shouted, finally breaking. "Stop!"

Reaching for the brake handle, Starke pushed it upward to engage the break. Mercifully the chain came to a halt, though he noticed her hand remained on the lever, ready to release it at any time.

"Where are my team?" O'Neill asked.

Iosif glared at him, teeth bared. "Engine room," he said at last.

O'Neill and Starke exchanged a look. "So they're still alive."

"For now."

The threat wasn't lost on O'Neill. Reaching for the satchel Iosif had been carrying when they captured him, he held it up. "What were you doing with this?"

When an explanation wasn't forthcoming, O'Neill nodded to Starke, who tightened her grip on the brake lever.

"All right!" Iosif cried out again. "I was planting explosives against the hull. Dmitry is going to sink the ship."

"Sonofabitch," Starke said under her breath. "The *Munro* will get here and assume the ship went down with all hands."

"And by the time they figure out what really happened, Dmitry and his buddies will be long gone," O'Neill finished, then turned his attention back to Iosif. "One way or another, you're staying in this room until our relief ship gets here, so it's in your interests to answer my question truthfully. How many charges did you plant?"

"Four."

"Where?"

Iosif stewed on that for a moment or two. "Engine room, port and starboard side. And two more in the forward cargo hold."

Before O'Neill or Starke could say anything further, Iosif's walkie-talkie crackled.

"Iosif, report," Dmitry barked, speaking in Russian. "Where are you now?"

When no reply was forthcoming, Dmitry radioed again.

"Iosif, acknowledge now or we come after you."

Picking up the radio, O'Neill held it towards Iosif's mouth. "Tell him you're still working on the charges, everything's fine. And keep in mind that I speak Russian."

Glaring at him, Iosif nodded, and O'Neill clicked the transmit button.

Taking a breath, the Russian weighed up what to say next, making his decision a couple of seconds later. "Dmitry, it's a trap!" he shouted. "I'm in—"

A second blow to the head knocked him down. Releasing the transmit button, O'Neill turned away, bristling with anger.

"God damn it," he growled.

"Are you still listening?" Dmitry's voice asked a moment later, having switched to English now. "I assume you are, Starke. Iosif was one of my best. You must be good to get the better of him. I respect that."

O'Neill glanced over at Starke. The young woman was staring at the radio, saying nothing.

"I will make this simple," Dmitry went on. "You will present yourself on deck within two minutes and surrender to us."

Swallowing hard, Starke held out her hand for the radio. When O'Neill withheld it, she looked up at him, her eyes pleading. "He doesn't know you're still alive. We need to keep it that way."

Reluctantly he handed her the walkie-talkie. Taking a moment to compose herself, she held it up and hit the transmit button. "And why should I do that?"

The response didn't come immediately. For several seconds, O'Neill and Starke stood there in silence, waiting for what their adversary was about to do.

The answer, when it came, was enough to send a chill through them.

"Kate."

The voice that spoke wasn't Dmitry's.

"Watkins?" Starke gasped. "You okay?"

"I'm sorry, Kate. The sons of bitches jumped me in the engine room."

"Tell them what I'm doing, my friend," they heard Dmitry command him. "Tell them now."

"He's got a gun pointed at me. We're on the bridge, Kate! We've—"

His voice was drowned out by the sharp crack of a gunshot, followed a second or so later by Watkins' howls of pain. Dmitry kept his radio transmitting the whole time so they heard every terrible moment of it.

"You get the idea, Starke," he said when Watkins' cries had subsided. "The next one is in his head if I do not see you on deck in two minutes. After that, I kill Rodriguez and hunt you down anyway. Decide now."

With that, his transmission ended, and a deathly silence fell on the room.

Then, just like that, Starke reacted. "Here, take this," she said, handing O'Neill her weapon. "Find those charges, Rick. Then kill that sonofabitch. I'll buy you as much time as I can."

With that, she turned towards the hatch leading out on deck. O'Neill grabbed her arm and spun her around to face him.

"You're not going out there," he said firmly.

"You heard what he said. He'll kill Watkins and Rodriguez if I don't."

"And he'll kill all of you if you do," O'Neill countered.

"Not if you stop him." She swallowed hard. "I have to do this, Rick."

Suddenly, she reached out and pulled him to her, holding him in a fierce, desperate embrace. His grip on her arm slackened as he returned the gesture.

No sooner had he let go than she slipped out of his grasp, disappeared through the hatch and slammed it closed before he could stop her.

"Kate, don't do this," O'Neill shouted, trying to unlatch it. It was no good; she'd jammed the lock. "Open the hatch!"

Staring at him through the small viewing port, Starke gave him a fleeting look of apology before turning away, hurrying out across the rain-soaked deck.

CHAPTER 21

DMITRY WAS ON THE *Ossora*'s bridge overlooking the deck below. He glanced at his watch as the two-minute timer reached zero.

"Your comrade thought very little of you, my friends," he said, turning towards the two Coast Guard men kneeling before him, their hands bound behind their backs. Blood was pooling from the gunshot wound to Watkins' thigh, but his moans of pain had been silenced by duct tape across his mouth. "Time's up."

He drew his automatic and leveled it at Rodriguez, who stared back defiantly at him. Brave but stupid. Such traits must have been common amongst their ilk.

"Wait! I see someone on deck," Yuri called out, pointing below.

Dmitry paused, turning to the younger man. "Searchlight."

Yuri nodded and hurried out into the starboard bridge wing, firing up one of the big directional searchlights that were mounted there to aid with navigation.

Making his way over to the bridge window once more, Dmitry was just in time to see the powerful search beam swing downward, illuminating a lone figure standing in the center of the deck. Wet, bedraggled, and pathetic-looking in the driving rain, it was the woman Starke.

Dmitry smiled. Had she stayed at large, she might well have caused more problems for him and his men. But just like her commander, she was gullible and weak.

Lifting his radio to his mouth, he spoke a single command to Oleg, who was on standby down below. "Bring her to me."

CHAPTER 22

DESPITE THE CHILLY AIR in the unheated cargo hold, O'Neill was sweating from exertion as he hurried along the starboard side of the compartment, his flashlight beam playing across the exposed steelwork of the *Ossora*'s hull until he found what he was looking for.

The Russian Iosif might have been a cold-blooded murderer by trade, but he was as good as his word when it came to revealing the explosives he'd placed. Perhaps his desire to avoid death had overridden his sense of loyalty to his boss.

Kneeling down beside the plastic explosive charge duct taped to the starboard side of the cargo hold, O'Neill carefully powered down the radio detonator, then peeled away the tape to remove the explosive charge. There was more than enough Composition-4 in his hand to blow through the compartment wall and breach the outer hull.

And there were three more charges still to locate.

Shoving the now inert explosive into the satchel he'd liberated from Iosif, O'Neill scrambled to his feet and hurried off to find the next one.

CHAPTER 23

"WATCH IT, YOU SONOFABITCH!" Kate Starke snarled as the big man Oleg shoved her roughly onto the *Ossora*'s bridge.

As she'd thought, his younger comrade Yuri was there, his blond hair now hanging wet and limp after his excursion onto the bridge wing. Kneeling in front of him, their mouths covered with duct tape, were Rodriguez and Watkins. The latter was bleeding from an untreated gunshot wound to the thigh, but both men were still very much alive.

How long they stayed that way depended on the man in command of the room. Dmitry had changed out of the grubby engineering overalls he'd worn when still pretending to be one of the *Ossora*'s crew, instead donning a black sweater and a thick leather overcoat that padded out his already muscular frame, and was standing beside the ship's wheel.

He smiled coldly at her. "Good of you to join us."

"I'm not here by choice," she spat.

His smile broadened. "None of us are. Tell me, what became of Iosif?"

"I killed him, threw him out through the anchor well," she lied, hoping his knowledge of the ship was as limited as it seemed, and that he wouldn't order a search for his man. "He's probably at the bottom of the Bering Sea by now."

For a moment, she actually saw a flicker of regret. "Pity, he was a good man."

"That's a relative term," Starke observed dryly.

Glancing at Oleg, the man who had escorted her to the bridge, Dmitry gave him a short command. "Open the cargo doors and get the container ready." This done, he looked over at Yuri. "Prepare the crane. I want the cargo on deck in five minutes."

As both men hurried off to follow his instructions, Dmitry turned his attention back to her. "You may not believe me, but I did not want it to come to this. My men and I were only passengers on this ship, hired to move a cargo. I am a businessman, not a murderer."

"You killed the *Ossora*'s crew," she said, anger simmering beneath the surface.

"That was unfortunate," he conceded. "But they became too curious for their own good, and found out our little secret. My orders were clear—if I was in danger of being discovered, there were to be no witnesses. I was left with no choice but to act."

"So what did you want with us?" she asked, knowing full well what he wanted. All she was concerned with was keeping him talking, buying time. "Why the distress call?"

He snorted in amusement. "For your ship, of course. My men and I could not manage a vessel of this size alone, but your boat will serve just fine. Enough for us to deliver our cargo to its destination."

"The Coast Guard will be looking for it," she hit back.

His smile returned. Reaching into his pocket, he held up the radio detonator that Watkins had used earlier to blow the engine room hatch. "Not if they think it sank along with the *Ossora*."

The loud clanking and rumbling of heavy machinery told Starke that something was happening on deck. Glancing out the window, she watched as the massive cargo hatch covers swung upward, propelled by hydraulic pistons and exposing the darkened depths of the hold below.

Standing by the bridge windows, Dmitry spoke into his radio. "Where is that crane?"

With his attention focused on the operation below, Dmitry had his back turned to Starke, allowing her to see the automatic shoved down the back of his jeans.

Realizing the opportunity that now presented itself, the young woman began to edge closer to him, one inch at a time.

"Moving into position now," Yuri reported.

She was getting close now. Her heart was beating fast and urgent as she prepared to act, a trickle of sweat mingling with the salty tang of seawater that covered her face.

Sure enough, one of the loading cranes on the port side was now illuminated, the tiny figure of Yuri visible in its operating cab. Slowly the huge metal arm swung inboard until it was positioned over the yawning hold, and Dmitry watched as the lifting cradle was lowered down into the gloom.

Now!

Starke rushed at him, already throwing out her hand to snatch the weapon from his jeans. As soon as she had it, she would open fire and keep shooting until he was dead or she'd expended the magazine.

But it wasn't to be. Seeing her reflection in the bridge windows, Dmitry whirled around, caught her arm and twisted it, using her momentum to force her forward into the instrument panel. She hit hard, banging her head against the sharp edge of a monitor, and felt blood begin to trickle from a cut over her eye.

Larger and far stronger than her, Dmitry increased the pressure on her arm and leaned in closer. "Did you really think I was stupid enough to turn my back on you?" he rasped in her ear. "I could snap your arm like a twig. Do you think I should do that, *Kate*?"

She groaned in pain as his grip tightened, but clamped her mouth shut and said nothing. Refusing to give him the satisfaction.

"Enough for now, I think," he said at last, pulling her other hand behind her back and using a length of duct tape to bind her wrists.

Once she was secured and no longer a threat, Dmitry released his hold. Starke collapsed to the deck, the muscles and tendons in her shoulder burning with pain as Dmitry resumed his vigil by the window.

"I want you to see this."

CHAPTER 24

THE CARGO HOLD, NOW open to the stormy weather outside, resounded with the harsh clang of metal on metal as O'Neill crept forward through the maze of cargo containers. He could see the chains and pulleys of a lifting cradle that had been lowered down from above. Clearly Dmitry and his men were planning to extract one of the containers, but why?

Creeping through the narrow, shadowy gap between two containers with the AKS-74 up at his shoulder, O'Neill came to a halt, surveying the scene beyond.

Sure enough, the lifting cradle was now in position over one container in particular, heavy chains attached to all four corners of Number 29. The source of the noise was Oleg, who was perched atop the container using a hammer and brute strength to force a pin into its shackle at the nearest corner. Huge and muscular, and swinging the hammer with practiced ease, the man seemed born for heavy manual labor like this.

Only his bandaged right hand gave some evidence of their earlier fight.

O'Neill would have to take him out. He glanced at the weapon in his hands, knowing it would be little use in such a task. It would surely kill Oleg, but the thunderous boom of an AKS round discharging would echo around the cargo bay like a bomb going off, alerting everyone on the bridge that something was wrong.

Gently easing the shoulder strap off, O'Neill laid the weapon on the deck as Oleg leaped down from the container and tossed the hammer aside now that it had served its purpose.

The big man was just turning to survey his handiwork when O'Neill made the decision to go for it, emerging from cover and rushing straight at him. There was no sense trying to creep up on him slowly. The patter of rain hitting the deck and roar of the wind overhead created enough ambient noise to mask his footsteps. His best chance was to close the range as fast as possible.

He almost made it, reaching within a few yards of his target before his foot caught a spare shackle that had been left lying on the deck, and sent it skittering across the metal surface with a clatter loud enough to echo around the cargo hold.

Oleg's head snapped around. Seeing O'Neill barreling towards him, he reacted immediately by grabbing his opponent and hurling him against the side of the container. O'Neill let out a cry of pain as his injured arm and shoulder took the brunt of the hit, white-hot pain searing down his left side.

"Still alive, bitch?" Oleg growled, advancing on him to finish the job. Massive and unstoppable. "Not for long."

O'Neill swung wildly, catching him with a solid blow to the ribs that would have doubled most normal men over, but not Oleg. The answering punch, though O'Neill managed to partially block it, was nonetheless enough to send him staggering sideways.

The Russian came at him again, swinging his massive hands like clubs. His fighting style was brutal, deliberate, and unsophisticated, but no less effective for all that. O'Neill blocked the first shot, but another came straight in after it, snapping his head sideways. He fell to the deck with stars dancing across his vision and blood dripping from his mouth, only for a thickly muscled arm to clamp around his neck, lifting him bodily up off the floor.

"I'm glad you made it back," Oleg whispered in his ear as he tightened his grip, cutting off O'Neill's airway. Already he could feel his vision darkening as he threatened to black out. "I wanted to see your eyes when I crush the life from you. Then I will do the same to your little bitch."

O'Neill lifted his right foot and drove it backward with whatever desperate strength still remained to him.

His aim was good, and he heard Oleg let out a growl of pain as O'Neill's boot drove into his groin. Suddenly the iron grip slackened and O'Neill tumbled to the deck in a heap as Oleg staggered away, moving towards a pair of shipping containers positioned closely together.

For a moment, O'Neill thought he might be trying to escape, until he spotted the distinctive frame of his AKS-74 lying between the crates.

Scrambling to his feet, O'Neill knew in an instant that he was too late to intercept the Russian, who had almost reached the weapon.

Instead he cast his eyes on the deck around him, seeking anything he might use to defend himself.

That was when he spotted the hammer that Oleg had so recently discarded, lying just a few feet away. It was a lump hammer, smaller than a sledge and designed to be used with one hand, but heavy and durable for all that.

O'Neill snatched up the improvised weapon and turned to face his enemy, just as Oleg grabbed the assault rifle in his meaty hand and swung it towards him.

O'Neill didn't think; he acted, hurling the hammer at his opponent and sprinting towards him, thinking the crude missile might at least disrupt his aim and buy O'Neill a few precious seconds to close the distance. He was already hurting and bleeding from their brief battle, but there was no other option.

He never got the chance to engage his enemy a second time.

There was a wet crunch, a breathless groan, and suddenly the big Russian's legs gave way beneath him. Dropping the assault rifle, he collapsed to the deck with an audible thud, unseeing eyes staring blankly up at the open sky above. A mountain of muscle and deadly strength suddenly rendered useless.

O'Neill stopped in his tracks, staring at the blood-covered hammer lying beside the crushed, gory dome of his enemy's head. Ten pounds of metal impacting at high velocity doesn't leave much to chance. He'd been killed virtually on impact.

Two men down.

Two more to go.

But first he had to find out what was in that container.

Kneeling down beside the dead man, he snatched up the blood-covered hammer, as well as the assault rifle, and advanced on the container. The pain was kicking in hard now, and he could feel warm blood from the bullet wound dripping down his arm, leaving spots on the deck as he limped onward.

The container was locked and secured with a heavy duty padlock. It looked intimidating, but it was made of nothing more than mild steel, and a couple of vicious blows from the hammer were enough to break the internal shackle. Yanking the broken padlock aside, O'Neill discarded it along with the hammer, and raised the assault rifle as he prepared to unlock the container.

Gripping the locking handle, he pulled it sharply upward and swung the door open to reveal the interior. The moment he did, his eyes opened wide in shock and the barrel of the weapon dropped.

"Jesus Christ," he gasped.

CHAPTER 25

FOR SEVERAL SECONDS, O'NEILL just stood there, staring at the sea of pale, blinking faces that confronted him. He saw fear in their wide eyes; fear and desperation.

There were so many. He counted at least thirty in sight, with more likely packed in behind. All young, all attractive, all female.

So many human beings crammed into that steel box, it was hard to believe. But they hadn't just been forced in there. He saw blankets and sleeping bags on the floor of the container, along with spare clothes and bottles of water and other supplies.

Somehow they had been living and surviving in there.

One of the young women pointed at the weapon in O'Neill's hands. He heard an exclamation in Russian, and a gasp of fear ran through the crowd. The ones at front tried to back away from him, only to be hemmed in by those behind.

Fear was quickly turning to panic, and if he didn't do something fast, this situation was going to get out of control.

"Is okay!" he said in his faltering Russian, keeping the gun pointed at the deck. "Not be afraid. I help. I am American."

That seemed to assuage their fears, but only slightly. Those at the front stopped and stared fearfully at him again, unsure what to say or do. Then suddenly a tall young woman with blonde hair, evidently one of braver ones, approached him. Her steps were tentative, but her expression was one of wary hope.

"Who are you?" she asked, speaking accented but fluent English. She looked him up and down, taking in his bloodied and disheveled appearance. "What happened to you?"

"My name's Lieutenant O'Neill, U.S. Coast Guard. I'm here to get you all to safety."

Her eyes lit up at this, but almost immediately they were veiled with suspicion. She glanced back at her fellow prisoners. "But what—"

"Listen to me," he implored her. "What's your name?"

She hesitated a moment. "Nika."

"Okay, Nika, here's the deal. You're all in grave danger here," he said, seeing no point in lying to them. "I don't have time to explain, but I need you to do exactly what I say . . ."

CHAPTER 26

UP ON THE *OSSORA*'S bridge, Dmitry turned away from the crane, now that its cradle had descended into the depths of the hold, and regarded the young woman who had tried unsuccessfully to attack him mere moments ago.

She was wise enough not to attempt such a move again.

"You never did ask me why," he prompted.

She glared back at him in impotent rage. "Why?"

"Why we did all this. What we were willing to kill for." He leaned closer conspiratorially. "Would you like to know what our cargo is?"

Starke shrugged. "Does it matter? Weapons, bombs, drugs . . . men like you don't need much of a reason to kill."

"You think we are terrorists or drug dealers?" Dmitry laughed. "Such limited thinking. We have something far more profitable."

"Like what?"

"Women."

"You're smuggling women?" Starke repeated, shocked by what she'd just heard.

He nodded. "Fifty-two of them. Worth over five million U.S. dollars."

"To who?"

Dmitry's smile broadened. "Anyone who wants to buy them."

The economics of such a scheme were staggering. Each young woman, sold into prostitution on arrival in the U.S., could bring in close to $100,000 before she was considered used up and discarded. The fifty or so they were transporting represented a huge investment that would pay off handsomely for his employer once they were delivered, and there were many more shipments planned.

All that was required were a few cargo containers, enough supplies and sanitary facilities to keep them in reasonably good health during the journey, and a ship captain willing to transport them without asking too many questions. Unfortunately they'd come up short on that last one.

"You sonofabitch," she said, appalled. "You kidnap young girls across Russia and sell them like cattle?"

"We do not kidnap anyone. They come willingly, thinking they are starting a new life in America. There are many young women eager to leave Russia these days. We even promise to have jobs arranged for them. Of course, not quite the jobs they had in mind, but such is life." He chuckled to himself. "Best part is, they even pay *us* to transport them."

Starke stared at him, aghast. "They're human beings, for Christ sake. Innocent civilians. How can you do this to them?"

Dmitry shrugged. He had long ago divorced himself from the moral considerations of his work, finding it best not to think of his cargo as human beings at all. "Not my problem. I am just a delivery man."

Dmitry fired up his radio once more. "Is the cradle in position?"

"I think so," came Yuri's reply. "I have tension on the wire."

He nodded in relief. A few minutes from now they would be off this fucking ship and on their way to the drop-off point with their cargo in tow. "Good. Bring it up."

As the crane went to work raising the container up from the cargo hold, gears and pulleys whining and clanking with the effort, Dmitry turned his attention back to Starke and grabbed her by the arm.

"Let's take a walk, shall we?" he said, forcing her down the stairwell. He paused for a moment before leaving the bridge, giving Watkins and Rodriguez a mocking bow. "Excuse us, my friends."

Emerging out onto the deck a short time later, Dmitry and Starke were just in time to see the cargo container descending towards the deck, swaying with the motion of the vessel.

"I thought you might like to take a look," Dmitry remarked as the container set down on the deck a short distance away with a resounding metallic clang. "Always room for one more."

Starke, tossing her head back to get a lock of damp hair out of her eyes, glared at him in hatred. "Fuck you."

He grinned. "Not me, but plenty of others will have you. Believe that."

His work completed, Yuri descended the metal ladder from the cab of the crane, unslinging an assault rifle from over his shoulder as he approached the container.

Dmitry keyed his radio again. "Oleg, get up here. We need your help transferring them to the Coast Guard boat."

Pausing for a moment at the door, Yuri gripped the release latch and pulled it, allowing the door to swing open. To his surprise, however, he didn't find himself confronted by dozens of frightened, desperate young women. Instead, he was confronted by yawning, empty darkness stretching out before him.

Darkness that was punctuated a moment later by the lightning flash of a weapon's muzzle flare. Yuri tried to raise his own gun, only to take the majority of the automatic burst in his chest and torso. Mortally wounded, he collapsed backward, his blood painting the rain-covered deck.

CHAPTER 27

STEPPING RIGHT OVER THE fallen man, O'Neill emerged from the shadowy interior of the container, the smoking AKS-74 up at his shoulder as he sighted his last remaining enemy.

Dmitry however had reacted quickly to this sudden change in fortune, pulling Starke in front of him, drawing his automatic and pressing it against the side of her head.

For the next few seconds, the two men simply stared at each other across the open expanse of deck as the rain and wind continued to whip past them.

"Not bad, my friend," Dmitry remarked at last. "I underestimated you."

O'Neill shook his head. "It's over, Dmitry. Your cargo's gone, your men are dead. Might as well surrender before you join them."

The Russian smiled coldly as he edged towards the port side of the ship, keeping Starke between him and O'Neill. "I think not. This ship is not where I die."

He had the shot. Starke was in front of Dmitry as a human shield, but she was shorter and smaller than her captor. O'Neill knew he could take him. But then, he'd known it last time as well. He'd been wrong then; what if he was wrong now?

The AKS was a powerful but inaccurate weapon, designed to be used en masse by Soviet infantry. It wasn't a surgical tool, but a sledgehammer intended to pound an enemy into submission. And if his shot was an inch or two off target, it would kill her.

O'Neill's eyes met Starke's in that moment, and he saw a look of understanding in them. She knew what he was thinking, knew the demons he was wrestling with, and she was trying to tell him it was okay. She was telling him to take the shot.

"You will lower your weapon and let me go," the Russian said, his voice calm and composed as he stopped beside the port railing, with the MLB somewhere beneath him. He was a man still in charge of the situation.

When O'Neill didn't flinch, Dmitry drew back the hammer on his weapon, the working parts clicking as they locked in place. "You hear that? I love that sound. It is so . . . decisive. It is the sound of your time running out, my friend. Choose now, or she dies and we both take our chances."

Take the shot, Starke silently pleaded.

For a moment, O'Neill saw it playing out. He saw himself pull the trigger, heard the roar of the weapon and felt the kick in his shoulder, saw Dmitry pull Starke in front of him and heard the sudden, sickening impact as the round tore through her skull.

"Last chance," Dmitry warned, finger tightening on the trigger.

"All right," O'Neill said, lowering the weapon and laying it on the deck. "All right. You got what you wanted, Dmitry. Leave—I won't stop you. Just let her go."

The Russian smiled, his gray eyes shining with malice. "As you say."

With that, he suddenly turned and shoved the young woman backwards. With her hands bound, she was unable to stop herself, and with a frightened cry toppled over the railing and disappeared.

"No!" O'Neill cried out, grabbing for the assault rifle he'd dropped.

But Dmitry had already disappeared over the edge himself, using a line attached to the railing to fast-rope down to the MLB below.

Realizing Starke would drown within seconds if he didn't get to her, O'Neill abandoned the weapon, sprinted for the rail and vaulted right over it, throwing himself into the darkness beyond.

CHAPTER 28

A SECOND OR TWO of terrible, sickening weightlessness was followed immediately by a crashing impact as he plunged beneath the waves. For the second time that night, freezing water enveloped him.

O'Neill kicked for the surface, breaking through seconds later.

"Kate!" he yelled, looking across the undulating waves in desperation. "Kate, can you hear me?"

"Rick!" a weak, desperate voice called out.

O'Neill glanced off to his left, catching a momentary glimpse of pale skin and dark hair before it disappeared beneath the surface. Immediately he kicked and pulled towards it. As he did so, he heard the MLB's powerful engines rumble into life, and felt the spray of water from the engine outlets as Dmitry accelerated away from the *Ossora*.

He no longer cared. Starke was his priority.

Taking a breath, he plunged beneath the surface, kicking downwards. Visibility was next to nothing in the inky darkness. She could have been right in front of him or a hundred yards away, and he wouldn't have known the difference.

Blindly he reached out, groping for anything solid but feeling nothing. His lungs were starting to ache as his oxygen ran out, his search growing ever more desperate. He couldn't keep this up any longer. She must have sunk beyond his reach.

There! His fingers brushed against something pliant. Some kind of material. *A jacket!* Instinctively he reached just a little farther, managed to grasp some of it, and kicked upward, striving towards the surface an unknowable distance above, just as it seemed that his lungs must burst.

O'Neill and Starke broke surface at the same moment with an explosive, desperate gasp, greedily sucking in air.

The young woman in his arms was coughing and spluttering, her hair in her eyes.

"Kate! You okay?" he asked, pushing locks of damp hair out of her face.

Then, to his everlasting joy, she smiled at him. "Never better."

O'Neill couldn't help himself. He let out a laugh of sheer relief, tilting his head forward so that his forehead rested against hers for a moment.

Only the distant sound of the MLB's engines prompted them to glance around. "That bastard's going to get away," she said quietly, watching the vessel depart.

CHAPTER 29

ON THE MLB'S ENCLOSED bridge, Dmitry was seated at the helm with the engines at full thrust. He was furious at the loss of his cargo, and the inevitable loss of profit for his employer. Likely this would mean the end of his career in Russia, as the people he worked for didn't look kindly on failure. He would have to go dark for a while, disappear, let them think he'd died along with the others.

But the world was large, and there were many opportunities for resourceful men like himself. In time, he would come back. And as much as O'Neill had thwarted his plans, the last laugh would still be his.

Slowing the engines a little, he fished the radio detonator from his pocket and glanced over his shoulder at the distant *Ossora* as he flicked back the arming cover.

Occupied as he was with escape and vengeance, he'd failed to notice the familiar canvas satchel stowed hastily beneath his seat.

"Sleep well, my friend," he said as he pressed the trigger.

CHAPTER 30

THE DISTANT ORANGE FIREBALL of the explosion lit up the sea like the dawning of a new day, followed by the great rolling boom as a couple of pounds of plastic explosive combined with about a hundred gallons of fuel oil.

Starke watched the fireworks display in disbelief, seemingly unable to comprehend how it had come about. It took her a second or so to realize what O'Neill had done.

"You switched the explosives," she gasped.

Despite himself, despite their dire situation, O'Neill smiled. "Best I could come up with at short notice."

It was Starke's turn to laugh, though her teeth were already chattering as the cold began to take hold. "Good enough for me. Now if you don't mind, can we please get the hell out of here?"

He wasn't about to argue. Turning back to the *Ossora*, he began to kick towards it while helping Starke to keep afloat, but it was hard going and he was already tired and hurting. The current which had drawn him along the vessel on the starboard side earlier was now pulling them away from it.

"This isn't . . . working," Starke managed to say, shivering violently now. It was clear she had mere minutes left, and he wasn't much better off.

"Just keep going," O'Neill said through gritted teeth, unable to believe that after everything they'd been through, they were going to die from exposure because they couldn't get back aboard. "We'll make it."

"You will," she said, looking him in the eye. "Go, Rick. We both know you can't get both of us back aboard."

O'Neill stared at her, wishing he had something he could say that would keep her going, but they both knew the truth. There was little to be gained by lying.

He knew one thing, though—he wasn't leaving her.

They were startled when something large landed in the water just a few yards away, showering them with spray, and stared in shock as Rodriguez suddenly breached the surface beside them.

"Hey, skip," he said, grinning at them both. "Mind if I cut in?"

"Seb," O'Neill gasped, hardly believing what he was seeing. "What the hell are you doing here?"

"You were tied up on the bridge," Starke added.

"I was," he agreed. "Lucky for you, I had a little help."

He pointed upward, to where dozens of faces lined the rails, staring down at the three of them. All young, all female.

"Now what do you say we get you out of here?"

In short order Rodriguez, reaching out with powerful and confident strokes, was able to help them over to the ladder, where a couple of lines were lowered from above and used to pull the exhausted O'Neill and Starke to safety. They were soaked, freezing, and bedraggled by the time they collapsed on deck, but still very much alive.

The young women who only minutes ago had been held captive inside the cargo container handed them blankets and dry jackets, much to O'Neill's amazement. They had just saved not just his life, but Starke's too.

As before, it was the young blonde woman named Nika who stepped up to speak to him, and he suspected she was the one who had coordinated the rescue effort. As one leader to another, he'd never been more grateful to another human being.

"We know now what those men had planned for us," she began, sober and serious. "You said you would get us to safety. That means all of us. Do I have your word?"

O'Neill looked back at her, understanding exactly what she wanted, both for herself and the fifty-one other young women who had set out on their hazardous, desperate venture. A chance at a new life.

"You do," he promised her, holding out his hand.

After hesitating a moment, the young woman reached out and took it.

EPILOGUE

Attu Station – Three weeks later

O'NEILL ONCE MORE FOUND himself in his office, staring at his computer screen. At least this time, there was no storm brewing, either outside or in the office itself.

The cutter *Munro*, traveling at flank speed far longer than her engineer considered safe, had arrived on the scene a couple of hours after Starke and O'Neill were plucked from the water. They'd subsequently found four Coast Guard personnel and over fifty Russian refugees in the mess hall, quietly drinking from a couple of bottles of vodka they'd been lucky enough to find. What the hell—they'd all earned it that night.

Boarding parties had managed to attach towing lines and escort the crippled vessel into safer waters, while medical teams tended to the injured.

Watkins' gunshot wound was healing up quickly, and some of the girls had been treated for illness and malnutrition, but all were expected to make full recoveries. Watkins himself had even grudgingly acknowledged that O'Neill wasn't as big of an asshole as he'd first thought, which was high praise indeed.

The team had attended a funeral service for Wyatt Richards. As relieved as they all were to have survived the ordeal, there was no escaping the grief of losing one of their own.

They had however gained some consolation from the intelligence provided by Iosif, the one surviving member of Dmitry's smuggling crew, who had been all too eager to spill his guts in exchange for a reduced sentence. His information had led to a spate of arrests both in Russia and the United States, dismantling a sex trafficking operation worth hundreds of millions of dollars.

O'Neill too had lived up to his word, pulling whatever strings he could to ensure that Nika and her fellow captives were granted refugee status and relocated within the U.S. He didn't imagine he'd ever see any of them again, but it gave him some comfort to know they'd finally found what they had risked so much to achieve.

And with the endless debriefings and excitement now at last calming down, the only thing that remained was to put his own affairs in order. The resignation email that he'd typed up what felt like a lifetime ago was still sitting on his computer, waiting to be sent. One mouse click would put it in motion.

"So what do you think?" Kate Starke asked, perched on the edge of the desk with her arms folded, a faint but knowing smile on her face. "You going to send that or what?"

O'Neill glanced at her, then back to the screen. A few weeks ago he'd been desperate to leave this place, desperate to escape his past, desperate to get out of the service. But a lot could change in a few weeks.

He certainly had.

Reaching out, he gently moved the pointer to the "Delete" icon, and with a single click, erased the email and the broken man who had written it.

O'Neill smiled, feeling lighter and younger than he had for a long time.

"Thought I might stick around a while longer," he said, sensing somehow that there was a lot more still to come, for both of them.

And he was ready for it.

Former Marine Corps colonel Amanda Collins and her lethal team have vowed to avenge her family's murder.

And they have nothing left to lose...

Read on for an extract.

Two years ago

WHILE ALL THE OTHER girls in kindergarten would doodle pictures of ponies and rainbows, I would draw myself parachuting out of helicopters and landing on dictators. My little stick figure would karate-kick twelve other stick figures, somehow making them explode in the process, and then I'd aim my portable missile at the obvious target: a dragon.

Nearly thirty years later, I'd be a Marine Corps colonel riding on a Huey. The only difference between the girl in my crayon drawings and the real me is that I didn't have a parachute, I'd use rope. And the dragon caught in my crosshairs wasn't a big lizard with wings—he was a little lizard with total dominance over the US–Mexican narcotics trade.

His name was Diego Correra.

We were midflight, northwest of Diego's location, which was a compound tucked in the outskirts of a Mexican town called Matamoros. It was nearly midnight. Dark. Hot. Damp. Eighteen members of my platoon were riding in three separate Bell Huey helicopters. Flying low enough to read road signs and fast enough not to bother.

I scanned the terrain below using the scope on my M16. The

goal was to spot anyone who might be on a rooftop with heavy weaponry. Was I scared? No. Was I lying to myself about not being scared? Yes.

We'd been hunting Diego Correra for three years. I personally had been assigned to six different raids on his drug fields and had been introduced to his legendary "business etiquette" firsthand. Yet I never got the pleasure of introducing him to my M16.

Our helicopters banked left. We were avoiding the city's population. It was a sizable town but not sizable enough that the growl of a chopper would go unnoticed.

The entirety of our intel came from an anonymous source who divulged only a single detail about himself: his name was the Fat Man. We knew nothing else about him. We had no idea if he was a defector from Correra's cartel or if he was the governor of Maine. *Fat Man?* I pictured a bloated, balding car salesman with crusted mustard on his tie, running to pay-phone booths with borrowed quarters to call me.

This morning he gave us the best news we've ever had. "Correra is in Matamoros. Tonight."

Two hours later, we were airborne. I kissed my kids good-bye and tried super hard to seem like a normal mom.

I'm not, though.

There are three main things that can go wrong while jumping out of a helicopter. You could get shot before you jump. You could get shot while actually falling. You could get shot after you complete your fall.

On this mission, we didn't anticipate there would be a fourth thing that could go wrong: your enemy kicks your teeth in.

I had on heat-protective gloves, but I let my boots absorb the majority of the work. I pinched the cord with the arch of one foot against the instep of the other. I don't know how the friction didn't cause a small forest fire, but, honestly, my boots have never shown signs of burn. Credit the US Marine Corps for that. Or me eating salads.

The ground greeted me like a speeding truck. *Wham*. Release, roll, get to position, crouch, aim, hold. Lieutenant Rita Ramirez hit the field second, taking front watch. She was my no-nonsense assistant team leader, so she'd be the caboose once our human caravan got going. Sergeant Kyra Holmes, the best navigator and the best shot, led on point as our sniper. My allies; my two best friends.

I'd never had less intel on a situation, and it was making me an anxious wreck, but my job as colonel was to win the Academy Award for seeming nonwrecked. The shrubbery up ahead was starting to afford us a view as we approached it. I could see the backyard of Diego's compound in front of us.

Showtime.

In general, this hombre used two to three roaming guards even when he was the visitor to a location. I'd have loved to believe these men would be his worst troops: the ones who drew the short straws and had to take the graveyard shift by obligation, the majority of their thoughts on whatever discount porn they might be missing out on.

But that's a dangerous assumption. These could be his best soldiers.

We divided into our three teams: two to engage from the sides and one to come over the back wall. Alpha Team, Bravo Team, Charlie Team.

Rita and I took Alpha toward the driveway.

Quiet and invisible. Those are the golden adjectives. We moved with as much silence as our boots would allow. No scuffling. No talking. Moving along routes that yield as much visual cover as possible. Bracing ourselves for the most complicated phase.

The entry.

Ideally, you fast rope directly onto a target, but Diego had used RPGs in the past: rocket-propelled grenades. So, no, the prospect of hovering in the air like a noisy piñata while angry men with rockets watched you from below was not desirable. Fifteen seconds up there would be an eternity. Too much potentially bad luck involved. No thanks.

My platoon didn't like bad luck. My platoon didn't even like good luck. We preferred drawing up two hundred different football-style diagrams with X's and O's, staring at maps and sketches, and letting everyone verbally shoot holes at our plans until we found one plan that seemed logistically bulletproof.

We passed quietly through the gate. And we arrived in the courtyard.

Already? Wait a second. This breach took no effort.

Oddly, this was the first sign that things were about to go horribly wrong.

The place was fully abandoned. From above, the compound looked like a normal set of buildings, but here at ground level, you could see this interior was hollow. Literally hollow.

Another group had already met us from the far end of their horseshoe-shaped journey. Bravo Team. We were all kind of staring at each other through a very empty structure: just some pillars and an old house with zero furniture.

"Bravo clear," said the Bravo Team Leader from a back room.

My heart sank.

"Charlie clear," said the Charlie Team Leader. Charlie had already arrived from the middle.

Is this over?

"Alpha clear," I said, barely able to hide the disappointment in my voice. I wasn't getting nominated for that Oscar anytime soon.

My platoon quickly began to scour the complex. There was nobody here.

Was the Fat Man lying?

And then Kyra found the first sign of what was to come: Blood. Lots of it.

I was thinking we had just executed the biggest failure ever. I was wrong. The failure was just getting started.

DIEGO CORRERA WAS MUCH more evasive than our mission budgets could handle. Some of our top Pentagon brass said he's just not qualified to be a priority, but during his rise to glory he butchered nearly twenty-nine hundred human beings, most of them innocent citizens, many of whom were children, with the worst aspect being *how* he did it.

It's a process he lovingly calls El Padron.

The first time I saw photos of El Padron, I threw up. I thought I'd seen it all. I'd been on over fifty missions in twelve years and led combat action in five different nation states, but I'd never seen anything as harsh as El Padron. It's like the guy was setting a world record for the most disturbing usage of pliers.

And there in that empty compound in Matamoros, I was about to get my first personal taste of it.

"Fat Man, this is Spider Actual. Do you copy?" I tried my radio on the off-chance that the Fat Man was patched in. "Fat Man, you there?"

He wasn't.

Kyra had blood on her sleeve from brushing up against a dark wall that was absolutely drenched with it. Fresh, bright red.

I began making my way to the roof of Diego's compound.

Something was wrong here. Very wrong. Yes, it's possible that Diego was tipped off ahead of time, but, beyond my annoyance at being evaded, there was a growing unrest in me. How can this place be literally empty?

"Fat Man, do you copy?" I said again as I climbed up the courtyard wall, grabbing a rain gutter to pull myself up to the roof of the compound. My goal was to scout the town from a high position. There would be a decent vantage point up there. I needed to at least "feel" the visual, to satiate my nagging need to see that there was nothing to see.

There atop the second story, I raised my M16 and scoped the horizon with its sight lens. "Fat Man, come in." I was hoping to snoop around whatever was visible a half mile down the main road.

I wouldn't need to look that far.

El Padron.

It was on our front porch.

The "message" was set up for us in front of the compound. At first I saw only one. But then I saw another and another. And by the time Rita joined me, there were twenty-three to behold.

Police officers.

All dead.

Two dozen Matamoros police officers, murdered, left in the street like confetti. Killed for no other reason than to tell us, tell my platoon, who we were dealing with. We were being warned.

"How can you be sure this is for us?" asked Rita.

"It's for us," I said, wishing it weren't.

"Colonel!" yelled Kyra.

She was calling me from below. She was already on the street, investigating. The other platoon members were slowly, quietly elbowing each other, calling attention to the spectacle out front.

Kyra was the first one to the center and she had found something she wanted me to see.

I went down. And I saw.

Each of the dead bodies was mutilated with an extra type of signature. It was known as Diego's Cross. He would etch it into the flesh of his victims. The wounds were fresh, the blood still trickling. His violently sarcastic artwork had taken place just minutes ago.

Minutes ago.

That meant our entire arrival was logged on their evening agenda. I grabbed the radio handset off our radio man. No more audio protocol.

Rita tried to slow me down. "Wait, Colonel." She was going to tell me there's no connection, no listener, no rational reason to bark what I was going to bark. But it didn't matter: I had already begun shouting into the void. "Fat Ass, I swear to God, do you have any idea what's on the street in front of—?"

"Tango, eight o'clock!" Kyra called out, dropping to her knee and aiming her M27 directly at the shadows behind us.

We all instantly spun around, took cover, and aimed, waiting for the silence to usher in a shit storm of trouble.

None of us lit up, though. Our potential tango, as in potential target, as in potential enemy, as in we're about to reduce you to burger meat, was a little girl.

"Hold your fire!" shouted Rita.

"Hold," I reiterated to my platoon. *We're not here to kill kids.* "Hold!"

The child was about nine years old. Unarmed. Alone. A local. She was emaciated but there was a raw energy to her eyes. She was driven by something deep inside.

She stood in the middle of the street and looked right at me, eye to eye. She knew I was in charge and I could tell she would deliver her message only to the one in charge. Undaunted, unabashed, she faced me directly, then raised her index finger and gradually pointed in my direction.

Slowly, viciously, she pointed at her own throat. She made the cross sign.

"Ya tenemos usted," she said with a carnivorous smile.

Then she walked away. Her words hung in the air.

We already have you.

ARRIVING BACK HOME IN Archer, Texas, usually felt good. It had been only a two-day jaunt, the Matamoros fiasco, but that's enough to feel like forever.

You miss everything when you're away. Everything. The traffic, the radio, the mini-malls, even the trash on the street. Why? Because that trash is hometown trash. That trash is made up of scraps of daily life. My daily life.

But nothing compares to the first glimpse of your front door. Both of my daughters love Halloween more than they love their own birthdays, so at this point our porch was covered with pumpkins and skeletons and Disney witches. Even though it was mid-September.

They were expecting me tomorrow morning, which technically was still five hours away, so I didn't want to wake them. I didn't even want to wake my husband. I just wanted to slide under the poofy sheets and reverse spoon him. To disappear into his dreams. True stealth.

He was a heavy sleeper. His fantasy football app would be the last thing on his phone besides one or two naughty texts from yours truly. He'd be out cold. Our hallway floor always creaked, so I took my time with each step. Nothing seems louder than walking to your kitchen at 2:00 a.m. I could even hear the fabric of my pants slide against itself.

I gently pushed open our bedroom door. We always sleep with it slightly ajar. Tonight was no exception. He'd learned over the years—the years and years of unpredictably long or short missions—that his sexy colonel could potentially saunter in at any hour of the night, and if he played his cards right, he could get that "she outranks me" sex he bragged to his buddies about. Though, on this occasion I was already spent, already shell-shocked from what my platoon had seen. *We already have you.* Drained from a day and a half without sleep. Tonight I'd be using him as a slab of warm comfort. He has his back to me. Curled in a fetal position. Perfect.

I crawled onto the bed.

And then my hand squished into a swamp.

A wet area of the mattress.

My first thought was that our eight-year-old was just here, napping, and probably had wet the bed. She'd probably left, stayed quiet, and thereby Daddy never knew. My second thought was that my husband had a fever and he was sweating out what had become a lagoon.

My third thought wasn't a thought. It was professional opinion.

My husband is dead.

I finally saw it. Bullet holes through his shoulder and through his temple. Heavy sleeper—they shot him in his dreams. His head was half gone. He'd been dead for at least three hours. *Who's they?* My legs were already carrying me down the hall. It wasn't even an instinct. It was like I was watching myself appear ahead of me. Fast. Inexorable. *Who's they?* Already bursting through their bedroom door. Already flicking up the light switch, already prepared...

To scream.

The training manual says to arrive at a violent situation and execute your training with dispassionate precision. Don't yell out your reaction. The enemy could still be nearby. Don't gasp. The enemy could get the first attack.

Don't let anyone know what emotional state you're in.

Keep quiet. Watch exits. Assess the scene. Keep your weapon up.

I did none of that.

My daughters were dead.

Both of them. Within several feet of each other. I grabbed my limp babies. The manual says to flee a situation where there is clear and present danger and insufficient intel. That's Chapter Nine.

What chapter is the chapter that says how to carry your dead daughters over to your dead husband? And place them in front of you, in a futile group hug, so that God could see that he might have made a mistake? That there is an undo button somewhere at his console he can press?

God didn't press it.

Diego's Cross was permanently etched on my family's flesh.

I made the only phone call my hands and my spinal cord were capable of making. I called Rita. I didn't speak. I couldn't. I couldn't make my mouth emit words. But she could hear my throat cracking in the air. She could hear all she needed to hear to know that this isn't Amanda's normal communication. And so Rita was gonna do what Rita would then do.

"This is your home phone?" she asked without expecting a reply. Calm. Decisive. Bankable. "Be there in four minutes."

Present Day

THAT WAS THE BEGINNING. That was what led me here to this freeway underpass, parked under a tree just beyond it, eighty miles east of El Paso. A million miles south of paradise.

Waiting. Watching.

I was in a sedan, waiting for the arrival of a particular truck. Rita was parked five miles away, watching from a small hillside. Page one of that manual I mentioned earlier says that heat is a state of mind. You can decide to be uncomfortable. You can decide not. I stopped feeling things entirely. It had been two years since I became a person without a family. At this point in my life, my skin doesn't feel. My skin merely assesses.

"Badger Three to Badger Eight."

I was talking to the Fat Man. I was using identification codes that intentionally misrepresented the size of our team. When your numbers are small, you want your enemy to think you are large. When you are large, you want them to think you are small. So says Sun Tzu.

I was no longer an active Marine. I was freelance.

"How's the road?" asked the Fat Man.

"Empty."

"What about the temperature?"

"Hundred and five," I replied. "About to get hotter."

Rita's voice then came on the radio. "Eyes on tango, Badger Three. Point-eight klicks. Barrel-assin' your way."

I looked up. I saw the truck. A big rig. Unmarked. Driving well over the speed limit, heading toward my position.

Time to rock.

"Good luck," said the Fat Man.

"Don't need it," I told him.

ALSO BY JAMES PATTERSON

ALEX CROSS NOVELS

Along Came a Spider
Kiss the Girls
Jack and Jill
Cat and Mouse
Pop Goes the Weasel
Roses are Red
Violets are Blue
Four Blind Mice
The Big Bad Wolf
London Bridges
Mary, Mary
Cross
Double Cross
Cross Country
Alex Cross's Trial (*with Richard DiLallo*)
I, Alex Cross
Cross Fire
Kill Alex Cross
Merry Christmas, Alex Cross
Alex Cross, Run
Cross My Heart
Hope to Die
Cross Justice
Cross the Line

THE WOMEN'S MURDER CLUB SERIES

1st to Die
2nd Chance (*with Andrew Gross*)
3rd Degree (*with Andrew Gross*)
4th of July (*with Maxine Paetro*)
The 5th Horseman (*with Maxine Paetro*)
The 6th Target (*with Maxine Paetro*)
7th Heaven (*with Maxine Paetro*)
8th Confession (*with Maxine Paetro*)
9th Judgement (*with Maxine Paetro*)
10th Anniversary (*with Maxine Paetro*)
11th Hour (*with Maxine Paetro*)
12th of Never (*with Maxine Paetro*)
Unlucky 13 (*with Maxine Paetro*)
14th Deadly Sin (*with Maxine Paetro*)
15th Affair (*with Maxine Paetro*)
16th Seduction (*with Maxine Paetro*)

DETECTIVE MICHAEL BENNETT SERIES

Step on a Crack (*with Michael Ledwidge*)
Run for Your Life (*with Michael Ledwidge*)
Worst Case (*with Michael Ledwidge*)
Tick Tock (*with Michael Ledwidge*)
I, Michael Bennett (*with Michael Ledwidge*)
Gone (*with Michael Ledwidge*)
Burn (*with Michael Ledwidge*)
Alert (*with Michael Ledwidge*)
Bullseye (*with Michael Ledwidge*)

PRIVATE NOVELS

Private (*with Maxine Paetro*)
Private London (*with Mark Pearson*)
Private Games (*with Mark Sullivan*)
Private: No. 1 Suspect (*with Maxine Paetro*)
Private Berlin (*with Mark Sullivan*)
Private Down Under (*with Michael White*)

Private L.A. (*with Mark Sullivan*)
Private India (*with Ashwin Sanghi*)
Private Vegas (*with Maxine Paetro*)
Private Sydney (*with Kathryn Fox*)
Private Paris (*with Mark Sullivan*)
The Games (*with Mark Sullivan*)
Private Delhi (*with Ashwin Sanghi*)

NYPD RED SERIES

NYPD Red (*with Marshall Karp*)
NYPD Red 2 (*with Marshall Karp*)
NYPD Red 3 (*with Marshall Karp*)
NYPD Red 4 (*with Marshall Karp*)

DETECTIVE HARRIET BLUE SERIES

Never Never (*with Candice Fox*)
Fifty Fifty (*with Candice Fox, to be published July 2017*)

STAND-ALONE THRILLERS

Sail (*with Howard Roughan*)
Swimsuit (*with Maxine Paetro*)
Don't Blink (*with Howard Roughan*)
Postcard Killers (*with Liza Marklund*)
Toys (*with Neil McMahon*)
Now You See Her (*with Michael Ledwidge*)
Kill Me If You Can (*with Marshall Karp*)
Guilty Wives (*with David Ellis*)
Zoo (*with Michael Ledwidge*)
Second Honeymoon (*with Howard Roughan*)
Mistress (*with David Ellis*)
Invisible (*with David Ellis*)
The Thomas Berryman Number
Truth or Die (*with Howard Roughan*)
Murder House (*with David Ellis*)
Woman of God (*with Maxine Paetro*)
Hide and Seek
Humans, Bow Down (*with Emily Raymond*)
The Black Book (*with David Ellis*)
Murder Games (*with Howard Roughan*)
Black Market

BOOKSHOTS

Black & Blue (*with Candice Fox*)
Cross Kill
Private Royals (*with Rees Jones*)
The Trial (*with Maxine Paetro*)
Chase (*with Michael Ledwidge*)
113 Minutes (*with Max DiLallo*)
The Verdict (*with Robert Gold*)
French Kiss (*with Richard DiLallo*)
Killer Chef (*with Jeffrey J. Keyes*)
The Christmas Mystery (*with Richard DiLallo*)
Kidnapped (*with Robert Gold*)
Come and Get Us (*with Shan Serafin*)
Hidden (*with James O. Born*)
Malicious (*with James O. Born*)
French Twist (*with Richard DiLallo*)
The Exile (*with Alison Joseph*)
The End (*with Brendan DuBois*)
The Shut-In (*with Duane Swierczynski*)
Private Gold (*with Jassy Mackenzie*)
After the End (*with Brendan DuBois*)
Diary of a Succubus (*with Derek Nikitas*)